AF256923

THE MYSTIC

12·21·12 - The Hate Apocalypse

Book 6

Jo Michaels

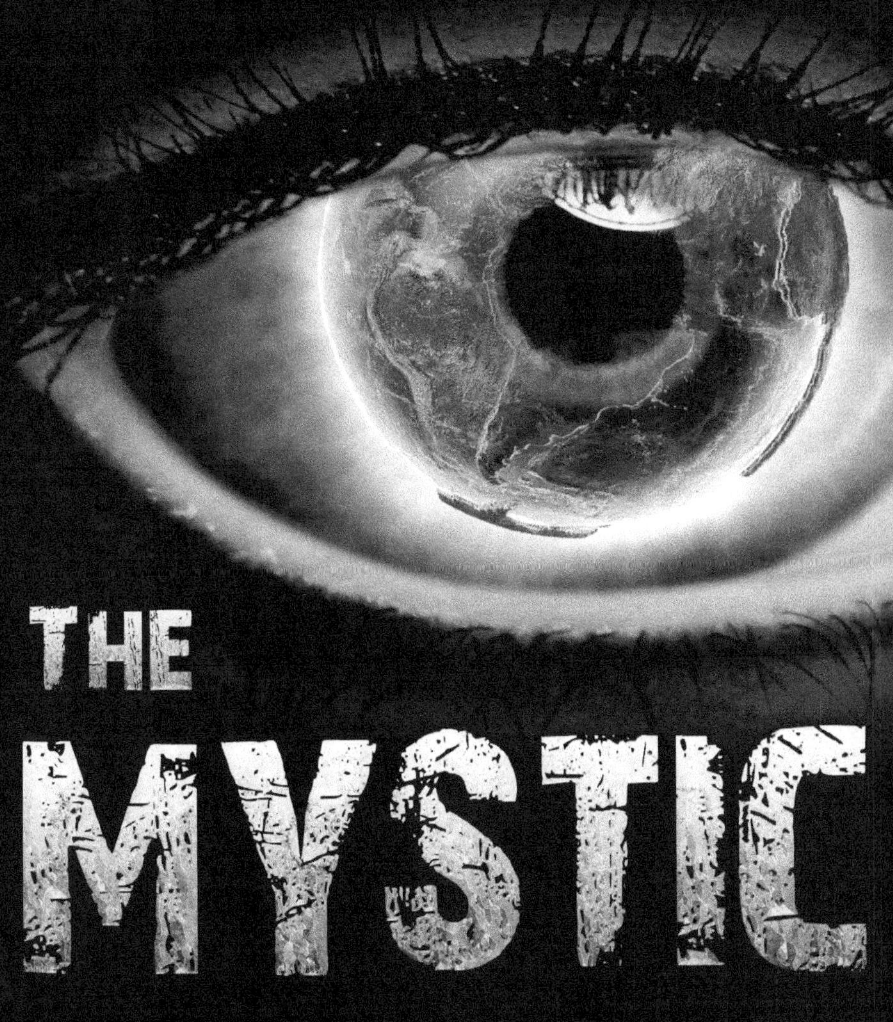

THE MYSTIC

12·21·12 - The Hate Apocalypse

Book 6

Jo Michaels

The Mystic

12.21.12 – The Hate Apocalypse – Book 6

By Jo Michaels

Copyright © 20189 Jo Michaels

All Rights Reserved

Published February 28, 2019

ISBN: 9781798213162

License Notes:

This book is licensed for your personal enjoyment only. It may not be copied or re-distributed in any way. Author holds all copyright.

This book is a work of fiction and does not represent any individual living or dead.

Names, characters, places, and incidents either are products of the author's imagination or are used fictitiously.

This book was previously published in 2013 with the title: Mystic-Markaza. Significant changes have been made to the story. Author retains all copyright.

Cover design by Jo Michaels

Typeset for print and digital formatting by Jo Michaels

The unauthorized reproduction or distribution of a copyrighted work is illegal. Criminal copyright infringement, including infringement without monetary gain, is investigated by the FBI and is punishable by fines and federal imprisonment.

Dedicated to all the women of the world who've felt judgment
or hate. May this book bring a smile to your face and light to
your heart.

CHAPTER ONE

BEING PSYCHIC

Markaza sat at the table in The Clementine's restaurant and chewed her food. Never in her life had she been so afraid of being alone. What if the monster's description caused the other young ladies of Women Save the World to abandon her? There was no way she could fly solo. She'd die; they'd all die. Goose-bumps lifted the hair on her arms, and she shivered.

They were bantering in their easy way, everyone seeming to feel deeply for the other after hearing their stories. Bronya being ostracized for being a lesbian, Lily and her self-image after the accident that left her scarred for life, and the other three, Shelia, Melody, and Coralie, all mangled or abused in some way.

Even though they were all damaged, each held a power that would determine the fate of the human race. Markaza hid her irritation over not being able to tell the ladies how to use their power, only help them discover it for themselves. She smiled as she watched Lily poke Bronya and point out the hottest woman in the room. Markaza's ladies had a bond that would, hopefully, be difficult to break.

She was staring at her Reuben sandwich and pile of fries when the room went dark.

Blood.

There's blood everywhere. It's on the ground, her clothes, and her hands. Screams shatter the darkness.

A disembodied voice fills the air. "You're next."

She woke to someone shaking her. With her butt still in the chair, she blinked and looked around the table. "What happened?"

"Girl, you just fell into your plate. You scared the shit outta me!" Shelia was as white as a linen napkin.

"Oh, sorry."

"What was that?"

"Nothing. Don't worry about it. I'm fine. I just need to eat. I think."

Shelia lifted an eyebrow. "You should probably start with the fries stuck to your face. Seriously, you okay?"

Markaza nodded. "Happens all the time."

"We know. But not usually in the middle of dinner." Bronya added. "I was about to make a scene if you didn't come back around."

Picking up a napkin, Markaza wiped her face—hyperaware of the ladies' eyes on her—lifted her sandwich, and took a big bite; smiling at the others to show she was fine. Once she felt like she had them convinced, and reassured them again, she thought about what she'd seen in the vision as she polished off her food. Blood—okay, that was a little creepy, but nothing to get too frantic over. Darkness—big deal, who cared about night? When she recalled the voice, she shuddered. That was the creature for sure. What the hell did he mean she was *next*? No one was dead.

Melody's voice intruded on the train of thought. "So, Markaza, are we gonna find out how you came by that swanky apartment, and why everyone here seems to know you?" She crossed her arms over her chest and smiled.

"Yeah. Is everyone done?"

A round of "yes" echoed from the others.

"Great. Let's get back upstairs. There's a lot to do and not a lot of time to do it in." Markaza stood up and headed for the elevator. She talked as they moved along. "That lovely brown lady you all know from the front desk is like a second mother to me. Well, like a first mother, really. My own is kinda sucky lately." A wave was given in Nancy's direction. The woman smiled and nodded in return.

"This hotel is mine. It would've been my mother's if her cheese hadn't launched off the trap when my dad died."

"The Clementine belongs to you?" Coralie's eyes were wide, and her mouth dropped open.

Markaza nodded. "My family has owned it from day one. I'm the one who turned it into what it is today: a five-star everything. We have the best of the best. No one on my staff steals or lazes around. Somehow, the canny owner always knows." She winked and tapped her temple.

They got in the elevator, and she pressed the button for their floor. "See, when people think you have cameras *everywhere*, they tend to behave themselves. Rumors spread fast through the staff, and once you catch someone doing something that was supposed to be on the sly, everyone else seems to magically fall in line."

When they stepped out on the top floor, she pointed down the hall. "My mother lives down there, in suite two. She doesn't come out, and only Nancy and one housekeeper are allowed in. When I saw Mom last, she didn't even know her own name. Maybe, if I can get all this shit that I'm dealing with right now sorted out, I'll have time to take her to a doctor or something." Markaza chuffed. "I think she's traumatized. PTSD or something."

She unlocked the door, pushed it open, and gestured for everyone to enter. At the questioning looks from the other girls, she continued. "You'll understand when I'm done telling you *my* story. Anyway, go get comfortable, and I'll meet you all back here in a little bit."

They scattered when they entered the apartment. Markaza went down the hall to her own room and pulled out a pair of cloth pants with the PINK logo on them, a soft t-shirt, and a bandanna. She wrapped up her hair, took off her makeup, and changed. Looking at her reflection in the mirror, she narrowed her eyes. "Time to tell them the whole story. Try not to freak them out too much." A wry grin was returned, and she spun on her heel.

Coralie and Lily were sitting next to one another on the couch, looking like they'd been friends since emerging from their mothers' wombs, when Markaza returned.

Lily giggled. "I really love this chicka to death! She's funny and awesome. I'm so glad she joined us."

Markaza gave them a smile. "That's wonderful. Hey, could you guys stand up for a minute and give me a hand?"

"Sure!" they replied in unison. It brought on another outburst of giggles.

If they don't stop that, I may throw up. Markaza hoped her face didn't betray her thoughts. "Let's rearrange the furniture in here. Move the couch over there, I'm gonna put my chair right here, and let's put the rest of them facing it, in a circle."

There was a flurry of activity as the seats were arranged so everyone could see Markaza as she talked. Bronya, Shelia, and Melody came in and milled around, looking confused.

"Lily, would you mind taking the books and putting them in my room? Also, there are two little baggies on the nightstand. Could you bring them here, please?"

"Yessm!" Lily charged down the hall.

"Bronya, I want you to sit there." Markaza pointed to the first seat to the left of her own chair. "And the rest of you please sit in order from the time you arrived here."

THE MYSTIC

They took their seats, leaving a gap for Lily. When she returned, she deposited the baggies in Markaza's hand and scurried to sit.

Slowly, Markaza made her way to her chair; feeling like the weight of the world was on her shoulders. She plopped down, closed her eyes, and took a deep, cleansing breath.

"I'm gonna start from the beginning so none of you get confused along the way. If you have questions, please, just ask them. I'll do my best to answer what I can."

Everyone was sitting on the edge of their seat. Some were tapping toes, some were drumming fingers. All looked nervous as hell, and all were nodding.

"Relax, guys. Sit back and listen."

Once everyone stopped fidgeting, Markaza began. "I was five when I had my first vision—looked like what you all witnessed in the restaurant a little bit ago. It was in my kindergarten classroom. Private, Catholic school, of course. My teacher freaked the hell out. She picked me up, ran to the office, and told them to call my parents to pick me up." She laughed. "I found out later that I'd fallen on the floor, my eyes rolled back in my head, and I told her that her dog was gonna maul her son 'in the voice of the Devil'—her words, not mine. Needless to say, I wasn't allowed to return to school there. I thought about it a few years ago and looked her up. Big news story. Her dog did end up mauling her son. Nothing serious, but the dog was ordered put down, and there was huge public outcry over it at the time.

"I don't remember many of my visions past that one until my sixth birthday party. I woke up that morning in a cold sweat and ran to my mother. I told her I'd seen my best friend, Mary, drown in the pool at the club.

"Mom reassured me it was all a dream, said Mary would be fine, patted me on the head, gave me a hug, and sent me to get dressed.

"Time for the party rolled around, and I'd forgotten all about my dream. Ice cream, a huge cake, and lots of presents are a good distraction for a six-year-old mind. Everyone sang happy birthday, I blew out the candles on the cake, and they oohed and aahed over my presents as I opened them. When it was time for everyone to leave, they found Mary floating face-down in the pool." Markaza felt her stomach lurch with the memory and prayed lunch would stay down. Her eyes burned. "I cried and started blabbing about knowing it was gonna happen and warning my mother." She felt the first tear roll down her face. "My mom stuffed me in the car and told our driver to take me home to Nancy.

"Unlike my never-gave a crap mother, Nancy listened and took me seriously. She told me not to tell anyone when I had a dream because people wouldn't understand. We decided to keep it between us from then on. Nancy never judged me and tried to help when and where she could. I went to her a lot after that. My mom was totally left out of the loop... Well, for the most part.

"Anyway, when I turned seven, a boy I liked broke his leg at my birthday party. It would've been a lot worse, but Nancy was there and watching over us. I'd had a dream he was gonna die and told her about it. She pushed him out of the way of the car in the nick of time, but she landed on him and broke his leg. That was the first time I considered being able to change the future.

"Every birthday was the same; something horrendous happened to someone I cared about. At first, I thought it was the parties that were causing the disasters. But I skipped having one when I turned thirteen, and it didn't matter." She paused. "That's one of my most painful memories. We haven't gotten that far yet, and I don't wanna skip time on you guys." Markaza shifted in her seat. "Let's see, where was I? Oh, yeah.

"When I was in fifth grade, one of my friends got kidnapped. Her parents were very prominent people, and the ransom demand was huge. They paid the people and she was returned; but she was never the same. Before it happened she was playful, sweet, and full of life. Afterward, she was skittish, rarely smiled, and was withdrawn. She killed herself when she was fifteen.

"My father considered all this and decided I needed to learn self-defense. He asked me what classes I wanted to take and, after considering all my options, I chose taekwondo.

"I was a natural. My parents wouldn't allow me to compete because they were worried I'd get hurt, but I didn't care. It was a release of my frustrations every day and helped me calm my mind."

Shelia piped up. "She's awesome. You should've seen her kick ass when those guys attacked me. I thought I was watching a judo ballerina."

"Yeah, I think you're the only one who's seen me fight in a long time; except Melody, in the parking lot at the mall." Markaza laughed. "I swear, that guy will never forget the beating I put on him." She rubbed her legs and tucked them under her body. She sat for a moment without speaking, pulling her thoughts back together. "Anyway, I trained for years. Once I hit age fourteen—which I'll get to in a moment—I was a force to be reckoned with. I was in the dojo one afternoon, not long after I switched schools, and a girl I'd sparred with on a number of occasions approached me. We'd had a friendly match earlier, and I had a blackout, something to do with some of the snobby brats at school plotting against someone I didn't even know. She asked me about passing out. I lied as well as I could, but she saw through it somehow; told me she had a gift. When I buckled and told her the truth, she gave me some advice on how to meditate and focus my visions. But I'm jumping ahead again." Markaza rubbed her face and backtracked.

"Okay, in the beginning of my sixth grade year, I had the first vision of my dad doing things he wasn't supposed to be doing. My mom and I were sitting at the table waiting for him to get home when the phone rang. She got up to answer and was gone a long while. When she returned, she gulped down her glass of wine and told me Dad wouldn't be joining us. He'd called and said he had a late meeting with some special out of town guests. I shrugged it off and ate my food.

"Later, when I was watching TV, I had a blackout. I saw my dad with a really pretty blonde. They were doing unspeakable things."

"Wait, you *saw* your dad having sex with a woman?" Melody blurted out.

Markaza nodded. "It was pretty ugly. Visions don't come with a rating, and there's no one there to filter them out. If they did, *that* one would've been triple X-rated for sure." She shuddered.

"Holy crap!" Bronya's face was bunched up. "What a gross way to walk in on one of your parents. I mean, we've all had an oops moment—or close call, I'm sure—but that's just not right."

All the other girls turned their mouths down.

"Tell me about it. Just wait; it gets worse." Markaza laughed. "Okay, yeah, so I saw my father behaving badly. This went on for two years before I had an idea and installed cameras in his office. Figured I needed proof to back up my mouth if it ever came to that.

"As you can probably tell, being psychic isn't all it's cracked up to be. I fell into a fit of depression at that point and was seeing a shrink weekly. I'd just had my thirteenth birthday. I think it's time you heard about what happened.

"Just like every other birthday, I had a vision the night before."

Chapter Two

Happy Birthday

Markaza woke up screaming. Her vision from the night before paralyzing her body as the horrors replayed through her head.

Sunny was standing on the tarmac at a small airfield, watching the instructor show them how they'd be tethered to the seasoned skydiver. She figured her face was lit up, her eyes sparkling with excitement, because she felt like a million bucks.

Markaza was inside Sunny, experiencing everything first hand. Her thoughts were as clear as a summer sky.

When the instructor showed the girls where the straps would go and how their tandem partner would have to hold on, her heart leapt in her chest. What a thrill it would be to have her body strapped so tightly to his! Antsy, her mind playing out sexy scenarios, she bounced from foot to foot, not hearing half of what was being said.

He paused. "Sunny, are you listening?"

"Yes," she answered. No! Rang through her head.

"Okay, let's continue." His lecture went on for another ten minutes before he finally told the girls to get their harnesses on and follow him.

Sunny stepped into hers and buckled the straps like she thought she remembered seeing the hot instructor do it. Satisfied she was good to go, she sauntered over to her friend. "Holy hell he's hot! Which one of us do you think will get to be strapped on to that?"

The friend giggled. "Maybe you will. It's so cool of your mom to sign us up for this for your birthday!"

"Right? I'm so excited!" Sunny's feet went into a tap-dance as she waited for the others.

Once everyone was geared up, they followed the instructor to a place where a group of young men was waiting.

Her heart started beating double-time. These dudes were as good-looking as the one who showed the girls how to get into the gear! She smiled and locked eyes with a boy who had brown hair that was almost shoulder-length, warm green eyes, and a perfect set of teeth. He smiled back, and she felt her face grow warm at the contact.

They were assigned their jump partners and, as luck would have it, Sunny ended up with the one she'd been eyeing.

He approached slowly, looking like a bronzed god, and her brain played scenes from every romantic movie she'd ever seen. Riding into the sunset, being swept into his arms and kissed, him professing his undying love...

"Hi," he said.

"Hey." She wanted to slap her forehead for being lame.

"You excited about the jump?"

She nodded, feeling like if she talked, she'd sound stupid.

While the other team members were getting ready, Sunny and her jump partner sat down and chatted, her voice finally able to return. He wished her a happy birthday, and she found out he was seventeen and had already made twenty jumps solo.

"Yeah, I just fell in love with it from the first time. This is only my second go-round with tandem, but I'm sure glad I'll get

to wrap my arms around you." His gaze was smoldering, and the ability to talk whooshed out of her again.

All she could do was smile while her inner-goddess danced and sang a happy song.

They climbed into the plane, and everyone sat down for takeoff. He grabbed her hand, caressing her thumb with his own as they rolled down the runway.

Roaring of the propeller was drowned out by her heartbeat echoing in her ears.

They reached jumping altitude and everyone was buckled to their partners. When he put his arms around her, she melted back into him. Instructions were being shouted over the din of the engine, but all she heard were his whispered words: "You smell so good."

At once, the door was opened, and the first pair of jumpers dove out. Screams of the young lady wafted back through the door as she experienced the first tingles of free-fall.

Sunny was shuffled to the opening.

"Don't be scared; I got you." He had to yell because of the rushing wind, but she was grateful for the reassurance.

She leaned over and looked down. Squealing, she jumped backward, making him stumble.

He put his hand over hers and pulled her tightly to him. When the boss yelled, "Go!" they tumbled out into the open air.

Wind.

Warmth.

His strong arms around her body.

Pure, clean air flowing up her nose.

Her hair blowing around her face.

Blue skies and fluffy, white clouds as far as she could see.

Electricity shooting through every limb, gathering around her stomach.

Brown and green landscapes, broken only by the appearance of the white dot of a house now and then.

It was the most beautiful thing she'd ever seen or felt.

When he squeezed her, she fell a little in love with him, and her entire body tingled. Adrenalin rushed through her veins, causing her to scream, "Wooohooooooo!" It was a welcome release.

She could hear him laughing as he let go of her with one arm so he could pull the ripcord.

A jerk.

Pain seared through her inner-thighs and down her arm as she was towed from his grasp.

Suddenly, she was falling again. She couldn't feel him near her anymore, and she grew cold. Her body flipped and bent in awkward ways as the speeding wind abused it.

A scream ripped from her throat as she plummeted toward the ground, completely out of control. Her heart did flips inside her body and caused her throat to constrict. Then, everything went quiet except the rushing sound of the wind. I'm going to die. *It was a perfect, clear, calm thought that was equal parts terrifying and relaxing.*

She quit fighting and was flipped upside down just in time to see the ground as it rushed at her face. Her body slammed into the concrete like a bullet fired from a gun.

Markaza buried her face in her hands and screamed again, letting her feelings flow out with the sound. *Death.* The word consumed her mind, and she recognized the agonizing fear for what it was. Never before had she been in the body of the person who died. She shook so hard, the bed banged against the wall, moving with her tremors.

Her mother rushed in, gathering the girl up, trying to console her. "What happened?"

"I… I… Where's Nancy?" Markaza screamed.

"I don't know! Can't *I* do anything?" her mother screamed in return, flapping her arms like a penguin's wings.

"No! Get her! Find her! Ahhhhhhhhhhhh!" Only Nancy would listen and not have Markaza committed.

An agonizing five minutes passed, during which she collapsed to the floor and cried, letting the sobs tear from her lips, not caring who heard.

Nancy arrived and sat down on the floor. "What is it, child? What did you see this time?"

Markaza threw herself into the woman's lap, wrapping both arms around her waist. "Oh my God, it was horrible! Nancy, we have to do something!"

Rocking the distraught child, Nancy used an even voice when she spoke. "Calm down. I can't understand you when you're hysterical."

Markaza gulped for air, taking it in as if she was being suffocated. Her stomach settled as her hair was stroked. "Sunny died."

"Baby, you've seen these kinds of things every year since you were just a little thing. What was different this time that's got you so upset?"

"I was inside her head. I saw what she saw; felt what she felt. I died, too," Markaza whispered. She pushed away and trembled again. It started deep in her belly and radiated out through her limbs, causing her words to come through chattering teeth. "She went skydiving and got severed from her partner when he pulled the chute open. We hit the ground… What do I do?"

"Oh my God." Nancy's eyes were wide and blank, her lips were pressed together, and her hand flitted up to touch her forehead. "I'm *so* sorry. I can't imagine…"

"It was *horrible*." Rapid breathing ensued, and Markaza could feel she was losing her grip again. "What do I do? If I call her, she'll think I'm a freak! She's the only friend I have."

"Let me think. Just try to calm down, okay? We'll figure it out." Nancy pulled the girl back up and embraced her. "Shhhh…"

They rocked for a long time. Markaza gradually relaxed, sure Nancy would know what to do next. After all, she'd saved many people over the previous six years.

"Okay, I'm going to call Sunny's mom. I'll tell her you said you knew Sunny was going skydiving but we decided to have a party for you and were wondering if she could come. That's all I can do."

Markaza nodded. "That sounds like a good plan. But what if her mother says no?"

"Then you'll have to call Sunny and hope she listens."

A knot of dread tied itself around her body, holding her prisoner, but she agreed.

Nancy pulled out her cell phone, got the number from the rolodex on the office desk, returned to Markaza's room, and dialed Sunny's mother.

"Hi, this is Nancy, I work for the Turner family?

"Yes, hi there. I'm calling because it's Markaza's thirteenth birthday today, and we've decided to throw her a party. I was wondering if Sunny—

"Yes, I realize this is late notice and she *did* tell me Sunny was—

"Yes, ma'am. I understand. I'm sorry to have bothered you."

Markaza's heart was bouncing around like it had been put on a trampoline. Looking at Nancy's face when she hung up and turned, Markaza knew she'd have to call and sound like the crazy person she was. She was sure it wouldn't end well. After pulling her thoughts together and calming her shaking hands, she picked up the phone and dialed Sunny's cell.

"Hey, girl! How *are* you? Happy thirteenth birthday!" Sunny sounded like she was smiling.

Markaza took a deep breath to steady her nerves. "I'm okay. Thanks. Happy birthday to you, too. Hey, I was thinking about having a party today. I know I said I wasn't going to, but I thought that maybe you could blow off the thing you were going to and come see me instead. We could make it a double party, and it would be epic." She tried to put as much cheer in her voice as possible.

"There's no way you're asking me to blow off *skydiving* to come to a party you just *decided* to put together, right?" Sunny laughed. "Have you gone crazy?"

"No, I just thought you might be able to re-schedule."

"What is it? Are you jealous because I didn't invite you to come?"

Girls could be heard giggling in the background.

"No." Markaza's heart sank and confusion set in. Their conversation wasn't going the way she'd hoped, and Sunny was being downright mean for some reason.

"Then why bother *suddenly* throwing yourself a party that you know I can't come to because I have plans?"

"I… I thought, maybe…"

"Seriously, what's really going on? Can't I do anything without you?"

"I saw you die while you were skydiving!" The words flew from Markaza's mouth before she could stop them, and she felt the pangs of regret rocket through her.

"Oh my God! You'll resort to anything! Girls, listen to this: Markaza says she saw me *die* while I was skydiving."

Giggles echoed in the background again and someone shouted, "What a freak!"

Markaza's blood boiled.

Sunny laughed and snorted. "You're so lame. Go have your stupid party with no one there. I'm out."

"Fine! When your fucking head slams into the ground, re-member I tried to warn you, bitch!" Markaza's phone beeped, signaling the call had been ended. She looked up, tears streaming down her face. "She wouldn't listen. I lost my temper. What can I do now?"

"I was afraid that was going to happen," Nancy said.

"Oh, you have no idea what I just did to myself. Now those cows in the car will tell everyone at school what happened. If Sunny dies today, I'll be a freak show. Not to mention I'll be losing someone I thought was my friend." Markaza started to shake again. "Guess I just did that anyway. Why does this stuff happen to me? What did I do to deserve this curse?"

"You can't look at it that way. Instead, think about all the people you've *saved* with your gift."

"Funny thing, I don't think they ever would've been in danger if it wasn't for me. It seems the people I love the most are the ones who get hurt."

"I'm still here and in one piece." Nancy smiled.

Markaza shuddered. "Yeah, and I'm trying to work out why that is. Of all the people I care about the deepest, you, Mom, and Dad seem to all be immune." She let out a sigh. "It's weird. You'd think you three would be among the first to get hurt."

Nancy laughed. "You sure have a way of making people nervous. Don't jinx me, okay?"

"Okay. Sorry. This thing with Sunny has my head all messed up."

"You did what you could. So did I. If people won't listen, it's not our fault." Nancy brushed Markaza's hair back. "Why don't I bring you something to help you sleep? You can pass the day that way. You need to calm down; your face is still all flushed."

"You're right. Okay. Thanks."

Nancy returned a few minutes later with some pills and a glass of water.

Markaza downed them and crawled back into bed.

"You want me to stay until you fall asleep?"

"No, I'll be okay." An odd numb feeling had taken over her body, and she wondered if she was experiencing shock. "I love you."

"I love you, too. Get some sleep." Nancy left, closing the door softly.

Markaza could hear her mother arguing with the woman in the hallway. They were doing their best to whisper, but the walls carried the sound.

"What's wrong with her?"

"Nothing. She just had a scary dream."

"Is she going on about those stupid visions again? I hear you two talking sometimes; you really shouldn't encourage her."

"I help her try to deal with what she sees. I don't know if any of it's real, but she believes it is, and I'm going with the assumption she's *not* crazy." Nancy's voice got rough and low, like she was getting angry.

"I'm taking her to a psychiatrist. She needs help."

"You do whatever you think you have to. She's your daughter."

"Yes, she is. You might remember that."

Everything went quiet and Markaza fell asleep, the drugs making her feel heavy and peaceful.

Banging on the door roused her from her slumber.

"Markaza, wake up! Get out here!" It was Mom. She was having a fit.

Markaza ground the sleep out of her eyes and rolled out of bed. Her head spun, and she sat back down.

"Are you up?"

"Hang on a second! My head is spinning!" After a moment, she was able to walk to the door and pull it open.

Her mother was completely disheveled. Hair that was usually perfectly coiffed stood in every direction, and mascara streaks—that for some reason went right into the wrinkles—marred her face, making her look *really* old. With her eyes as big as hula-hoops, she leaned down and whispered, "You have to come see what's on television." Alcohol wafted from her body and caused Markaza to gag.

"Geeze, Mom, how much have you had to drink?"

"Not nearly enough. Come *on*." Mom grabbed Markaza by the hand and dragged her to the living room. "Look at that. It's on every channel."

A reporter was holding papers in his hand and looking at the camera with a gloomy expression. "It seems to have been incorrectly used equipment that cost this young woman her life."

They cut to a video where a tiny figure could be seen plummeting from the sky.

"Her tandem partner said the buckles weren't fastened properly. You can see in the video how she's jerked up for a moment when the chute opens, but falls away from him when it begins to slow their descent. Let's watch it again."

It was rewound and played back, this time showing the entire grisly scene. When the parachute opened, one body was flung away from the person it was attached to, and it went spiraling out of control before slamming headfirst into the ground.

"They say her name was Sunny Carter, daughter of Melanie and James Carter, the finance mogul from New York, New York. She turned fourteen years old today. We'll bring updates as the investigation…"

Markaza fled down the hallway and dry-heaved over the toilet before passing out on the tile.

***

"When I woke up, my mother asked me if Sunny's death was what I'd seen. I told her it was, and I ended up at a psychiatrist's office that same night. He put me on a bunch of pills that made me groggy and skewed my visions. I went months feeling like a zombie. I'm kinda surprised I didn't walk around moaning and drooling all over myself. It was the first time I was heavily medicated for what they called depression." Markaza paused and blew her nose. "Who the hell wouldn't be freaked out? Geesh. Because of that little fiasco, I was bullied at school so badly, my parents had to pull me out and send me somewhere else. Not that I cared. I was too drugged up, and busy avoiding the visions of my father that had started, to notice.

"That's how I ended up at Her Majesty's Other Preparatory Academy—which we New Yorkers lovingly call Hemop. Those years were some of the best, and the worst, of my life."

"So, your mom thought you were crazy because you saw the death of someone and had the gumption to try and stop it?" Lily's voice rose as she asked the question.

Markaza nodded.

"That's more like hero stuff in my opinion. What a bitch!"

"Yeah, well, she didn't really understand, did she?"

"Still. Argh!"

"How about we take a little break before I get into life at Hemop?"

Everyone agreed, and Markaza ordered dinner to be sent up.

Nancy pushed a cart into the room an hour later.

All the girls hugged the woman and thanked her for being awesome.

She smiled at them. "Markaza's been telling her tales, I see. You ladies doing okay?"

"We are," answered Melody. "Thank you so much."

"Good." Nancy turned. "Markaza, we need to talk. It'll wait until tomorrow, but I wanted to let you know." Her voice lowered. "It's about your mother. Everything's okay, I think, but you need to know what she's been up to the last couple of days."

"Okay. I'll come down first thing in the morning. There's some business stuff I want to discuss with you, too. Thanks." Markaza hugged the woman and ushered her out the door.

After the girls ate dinner, they gathered in the living room once again with a huge pot of coffee and a bonus tray of fruit and veggies, courtesy of Nancy.

"Where was I?" Markaza asked.

"Ooh! You were gonna tell us about the shrink, the meds, and life at Hemop." Coralie was sitting forward, looking eager for more. "I've heard of that school. Always wondered what it was really like." She grinned.

"I promise not to leave out any of the gritty details."

"Great!"

Melody swatted Coralie on the leg. "Shhhhh! Go on, Markaza."

"Hemop is the priciest school in New York State and is K through twelve. My parents were trying to avoid sending me there because they wanted me to hobnob with more 'down to earth' kids—or so they said. Let me tell you, Mom and Dad weren't crazy. Those were some of the strangest teenagers I've ever met.

"It was like they'd never been real kids and were born as adults. They had perfect hair, perfect clothing, and perfect grades. Besides those attributes, they also knew perfectly how to manipulate people and make life impossible. I went to school with the president's daughter, the vice president's son, and tons of movie star offspring.

"Because I started in the middle of sixth grade, everyone wanted to know where I came from the minute I set foot in the door. It was like *I* was famous.

"I also got my first period right before I transferred. Talk about dealing with a lot of shit! Ha!

THE MYSTIC

"Of course, it didn't take me long to realize, if I was going to survive, I had to pretend to be something I wasn't."

CHAPTER THREE

HEMOP

Markaza took a seat near the back of the classroom and prayed the teacher wouldn't make a big deal out of the newest student in the room. Those prayers went unanswered.

"Class, we have a new student with us today. Her name is Markaza Turner." He looked over his glasses. "Markaza, would you please stand up?"

On shaky legs, she rose from her desk and lifted a hand.

"Want to tell us a little bit about yourself?"

"Um… My name is Markaza, and I just transferred here from another school. My parents own The Clementine. I'm thirteen."

"Well, welcome to the class, Markaza. You can have a seat."

She got back in her chair as quickly as she could and angled her head down, staring at the top of the desk.

"Try and follow along as well as you can. Come to me after class, and I'll see what I can do to get you caught up." His gaze diverted to the whiteboard.

Paying attention to the teacher was difficult because her last school covered everything he was talking about months before. Instead of following along, she panned her eyes over the other students.

All of them were wearing the same uniform she was, but theirs looked tidier, as if they were expecting to be photographed at any moment. Every one of the girls had a grown-up hairstyle and was wearing perfectly applied makeup. No one had pigtails, and braids and ponytails were done without a hair out of place. Guys all had short hair in various styles, but each of them was impeccably groomed. There were perfect creases in pants and wrinkle-free pleats on skirts. Not a single shoe had a scuffmark; it felt so formal.

She slid down in her chair and smoothed her own clothing, wishing she had some kind of makeup on.

At lunch, she sat alone and picked at her food. Every teacher seemed to have dated material, which made it hard to concentrate, and she bolted for the exit when the final bell rang.

Once back in the safety of her room, she sat down at her vanity and stared in the mirror. Her hair was thick, wavy, and dark, but hung limp around her shoulders. She leaned forward and studied her face, deciding she was passable but would wear makeup if it would help her fit in.

Mom had been sitting in the living room when Markaza came in and she made her way back down the hall.

"Hey, Mom?"

"Yes?" Pamela's nose didn't come out of the magazine she was reading.

"Would you mind if I went down to the salon to get my hair done?"

Without looking up, Mom answered, "Sure. I'll call and let them know you're coming. My credit card is in my purse; get what you need, honey."

Excitement shot through Markaza. "Awesome. Thanks!" She raced to get the Visa and hoofed it out the door.

Half an hour later, she was sitting in the chair, her stylist flitting about, mumbling about teenagers not taking care of themselves.

"What kind of stuff should I be doing?"

As though the woman just realized someone was actually attached to the hair she was fussing over, she looked in the mirror. "Seriously?"

"Uh huh. My mom and I don't really talk about it. Do you have any suggestions for a cut or how I should take care of it and style it?"

"Do I ever! You have beautiful hair; it just needs some TLC." She went to work, talking a blue streak as she cut, dyed, washed, ironed, and dried. By the time she was done, Markaza didn't recognize her own reflection in the mirror.

"Holy crap! It looks amazing!" Soft, dark brown layers with honey colored highlights framed her face and fell in perfect curls down her back, just past her shoulders. "I look so grown up!"

"If you follow the instructions I gave you, it'll look like that all the time. And I want to see you back every four weeks, okay?"

Markaza nodded. "Yes, ma'am." She ran a hand through her hair, reveling in its softness. "Yay! Now, do you have a makeup person around here? Maybe a manicurist, too?"

"Of course we do. We're a full-service salon."

By the time she stepped out the front door, she'd put a hefty charge on the Visa and had everything she needed to fit in with the kids at Hemop.

Her mother gasped when Markaza walked through the door. "Wow, honey! You look amazing!"

She felt herself blush. "Thanks. Can we start sending my uniforms with your clothes to the cleaner? I'd like them starched."

"Of course we can." Mom gave Markaza a hug. "This is such a happy day for me! You're finally growing up!"

Ew. Mushy stuff from Mom. Gag. Her arms wanted to push the woman away, but it felt kind of good to be held by her— even if she was gushing like a dodo. "Okay, okay. Enough of all that."

Mom's voice dropped to a whisper, as though there were someone else in the house that might hear what she was about to say. "Are you still *seeing* things?"

"Nope. Nothing." Markaza crossed her fingers behind her back as she lied.

"Good. We have an engagement to attend for your father tomorrow night. Why don't you wear that new dress I got you?"

"Why do I have to go?"

"Because you're our daughter. Now that you're looking more presentable and are adjusting to the meds… Well, I thought you might want to show people how normal you really are."

"You mean you want to show off your trained monkey."

"Markaza, don't speak to me like that. You know there've been rumors since your birthday. I just thought we could show people the real you."

Markaza snorted. "Okay, *Mom*." *Real me, my ass. You mean now that I look like a clone.*

"Good. Now, go along to your room. I'll have one of the maids come in and press your clothes for tomorrow."

It was amazing to Markaza how her happy bubble could be burst so quickly. She stomped down the hall and took a shower, being careful not to wet her hair, before climbing into bed.

On her second day at Hemop, Markaza was approached by a tall redhead with beautiful, alabaster skin that seemed only to enhance the smattering of freckles on it.

"You clean up nice," the girl said, holding her head high. "Elaine Wood; nice to meet you."

"Markaza Turner; nice to meet you, too."

"I know who you are. You stood out like a sore thumb yesterday. No one could help but notice."

Markaza cringed.

"Anyway." Elaine sniffed. "I'm having a party this Friday, and some of the girls want to meet you. Here's the address. I'll see you there." She handed over a printed linen invitation, turned around, and sauntered away.

Well! Aren't we just the cat's meow? Markaza stuffed the invitation in her bag and ran to the gym. At lunch, she was mobbed by a number of people from her class. They all wanted to know everything about her.

She lied and told them how perfect her life was and how excited she was to meet all of them.

Many of them showed up at her father's gala, strengthening her lie when they saw how her mother and father fawned all over their daughter. Every day at school that week was more of the same. A few people she liked, but most were as plastic and empty headed as the dolls they resembled.

She even sent an RSVP to Elaine's party. When Friday rolled around, Markaza gussied up and headed to the girl's house.

There was a line of limousines down the driveway and elegantly dressed teens were stepping out when the drivers opened the doors.

Thank God, I wore my Prada, thought Markaza.

Inside the grand house, everyone milled around sipping punch, chatting, and shaking hands. It seemed, again, as if everyone was already an adult.

A short girl with a light brown bob, sparkling blue eyes, and a megawatt smile approached. "Hi! I'm Renee. Elaine asked me to keep a lookout for you and bring you to the study when you arrived. Let's go!" She took off so quickly, Markaza had to run to catch up.

"Isn't it considered rude not to greet your guests at the door?" Markaza whispered.

Renee turned around and glared. "No. This isn't a formal event; just a casual get together."

"Oh. Sorry." Markaza wondered how people would be dressed for a formal event if that were a casual one.

In the study, there sat at least twelve girls with drinks in their hands. A few were smoking cigarettes.

Renee stepped forward. "Here she is!"

Markaza felt like a bug under a jar and wished she had a plausible excuse to leave. *No. They'll smell fear like vultures smell death.* Instead, she walked forward and stuck her arms out to each side. "I know you're all dying to learn everything about me. Who's first?"

A couple of the girls giggled.

"I want to know why you ended up at Hemop. Usually, unless you go there from day one, you can't get in—or don't want to." Elaine's eyes narrowed.

"Are you kidding? I've been begging my parents to send me there forever. They only agreed now because." Markaza lowered her voice. "I really shouldn't be telling you this, but *drugs* became a serious problem at my last school. A bunch of kids were expelled."

Elaine laughed. "Is that all?"

Markaza's widened her eyes. "Isn't that enough?"

"What? Do you live under a rock? Everyone uses something. Most people are just smart enough not to get caught."

"Really?"

"Yes, really. Here, have one of these." Elaine held out a cigarette. "It'll take the edge off. You look nervous."

"Um…"

Dirty looks were fired Markaza's way.

"Okay, thanks." She reached out and took it. A lighter was shoved into her hand.

They were all watching her.

So, this is the first test. Her hands shook as she lit the cigarette and inhaled. Every muscle in her chest screamed with the desire to cough the noxious smoke out. But she kept going like it was something she'd done every day of her life. She got dizzy after a minute and thought she might like the feeling. It was relaxing. When she was done, the girls acted as if they'd known her their whole lives.

She'd passed their little exam with flying colors.

Three weeks later, Markaza stopped taking the medication prescribed by the shrink, telling her mother it wasn't needed anymore. It seemed an acceptable replacement had been found; something that didn't leave Markaza drooling. Her visions became clearer, and she often shocked the girls with her knowledge of their classmates. They all wondered how she got the inside scoop. When they'd ask, she'd just wink and wiggle her eyebrows.

There was no end to the parties. Markaza was invited to every single one. Though she was careful not to forge close friendships, the others allowed her into their inner circle. She carefully refrained from drug use, knowing it wouldn't take much to get hooked. Carefully, she navigated through the rest of sixth grade and into seventh.

On Markaza's fourteenth birthday, Elaine ended up in the hospital. She'd fallen down a flight of stairs when her heel snapped and barely escaped a broken neck. Thank goodness, Markaza was standing nearby and was able to grab the girl as she fell. A broken ankle and a number of bruises were all that resulted.

Every morning, the girls in Elaine's clique met for cappuccino before school in the posh cafeteria. They'd sit on the brocade couches, nibble their breakfasts, and bash people outside the circle of friends. Markaza didn't say too much during these sessions, and her visions became clouded with plots against some of the other girls at school.

She withdrew from the group not long after she turned fifteen—the party where a boy she'd started to like crashed his car into the front of the hotel—choosing to keep to herself rather than be associated with the clique she'd once adored being part of. It was like with age came even more meanness, and she wanted no part of it.

Sometimes, she'd find herself inside the head of the targeted girl or guy, and it made her all the more leery of the "perfection" that was Elaine.

During the constant battling at school, Markaza also had to deal with what was going on at home. Her father's outlandish behavior worsened—something she loathed witnessing but couldn't stop—and it was becoming rare to see him at home. She had cameras installed at his offices, thinking about him getting caught up in some relationship or another and ending it with her mother, taking everything they'd built together over the years. Mom had obviously started to get suspicious because she cried frequently and had begun to drink often.

It got to the point Markaza dreaded going home. She spent more time at the dojo training and got her first tattoo. It was a bright red skull and crossbones on her upper-left arm.

Not long after, her clique deserted her for reasons unknown—probably because she quit feeding them information and hanging out so often—and she became a target for their cruel antics. They'd hide snakes in her desk, put bloody sanitary napkins over the handle of her locker, and yell stupid things while she was walking down the hall.

It was pure coincidence she discovered her ability to manipulate people. In the bathroom one day, she ran into Renee.

"Oh, look who it is! The *good* girl." Renee snarled.

Markaza's body tingled, and she turned around. "Why don't you go crawl back up Elaine's ass where you belong!"

Renee's eyes got glassy, and she walked out of the bathroom.

Shrieks sounded down the hallway, and Markaza ran to see what was going on. She burst out laughing when she saw Renee on the floor, trying to climb under Elaine's skirt.

For the first time in a long time, Markaza felt powerful. It radiated through her. That night, she had blue streaks put in her dark hair and got her second tattoo, a dragon, on her right arm.

Renee avoided Markaza like the plague after the bathroom incident; but the taunts at school got worse. People started calling her a witch.

Intrigued, she went to the library and researched witchcraft. While it didn't appeal to her, some of the instructions in a book on psychic ability for focusing the mind and working protective charms caught her attention. She bought herself a crystal ball and told her father she wanted to drop out.

***

"And he let you quit? Just like that?" Bronya asked.

"No. He threatened to make my life hell for it. You know, I tried for years to give him business advice, but he treated me like an idiot child; telling me how cute it was I imagined knowing what was going on in the business world. After a while, I stopped telling him anything.

"When I revealed I had inside information about why he was never home—and the proof to back my mouth up—he caved. After I showed it to him, I locked that shit up in a safety deposit box under a pseudonym." Markaza laughed but suddenly grew solemn. "He was such a bastard. But he was my dad, and I do love him." She shook her head and took a deep breath.

"Now, for my sixteenth birthday, I planned a huge party and invited a bunch of people I'd met at parties and the dojo rather than the snobs from Hemop. I also quit dressing like a princess. My mother was *not* happy."

CHAPTER FOUR

BITTER SIXTEEN

Springing from the bed, Markaza did a little dance. It was her sixteenth birthday, and she hadn't had a vision the night before.

It was such a lovely change, she sang her way to the breakfast table where her mom had laid out a huge spread of pancakes, sausage, and eggs.

"Wow! Did you do all this?" Markaza's mouth watered.

Mom cocked an eyebrow. "When was the last time you saw me cook?"

"Good point."

That meant she ordered from downstairs.

Markaza shrugged and fell to.

"Your father said he'd be home in time for your party. Are you excited?"

"Hell yes I'm excited. Thrilled, actually. I can't wait to party with my real friends."

"About that. I'm not sure you should be hanging out with those kids. They're weird."

"They like me for who I am, not what I look like, or what I can do for them. Back off." Markaza stabbed a piece of pancake and waved the fork around. "We don't bother you."

"But, honey, you've just changed so much. Smoking, tattoos, your clothes; the list goes on and on. Look at that neck thing! How will you hide it?"

For the first time, Markaza noticed her mom was fidgeting—something she frowned upon. "Are you okay?"

"No, I'm not okay. I'm worried about you, and I had a horrible dream last night." Mom sipped her tea. "I'm trying to forget about it. Please, let it go. I'll be fine."

At the mention of the word "dream" Markaza's stomach flipped. She wanted to ask more, but decided to do as she was told and let it go. "Whatever you say. But this is my party, and I've already invited everyone."

They stared at one another for a long time.

"Fine. Have your party. But things are going to change around here afterward."

Markaza shrugged, finished the amazing breakfast, and retired to her room to get dressed. They had to start letting the decorators in soon, and she didn't want to be lounging around in pajamas when they arrived.

A ringing signaled someone at the door a few hours later. Pandemonium ensued as caterers, decorators, and a cleaning crew descended upon the penthouse suite.

Thrilled, Markaza watched as the rooms were transformed. Their foyer became a grand entrance hall with streamers in gold and silver hanging from every available space. A crystal punch bowl—that was big enough to swim in—was brought to the dining room and filled with red liquid out of buckets. Huge ice balls with tiny, glittering fairies suspended in them were tossed in. Assembled in the living room was a dance floor, along with a stage for a live band.

She clapped her hands and bounced up and down when the cake arrived. Mom had spared no expense. It was five blocky layers of sparkly gold and silver gift boxes stacked on top of one another at strange angles.

Everything matched her party dress, and she rushed away to put it on and apply her makeup before the first guests arrived.

By the time the bell rang again, signaling the arrival of the first friend, Markaza was made up and ready to go. She stepped out of her room and sashayed down the hall in her new five-inch heels.

Mom's eyes popped wide open, and her hand flew to her chest. "What are you wearing?"

"The dress you bought me. Like it?" Markaza gave a little twirl.

"That monstrosity is *not* the dress I bought!"

"Yeah, it is. I just made some minor alterations. Well, I had it done."

"You are *not* wearing that." Mom's face had already gone through six shades of red and was bordering on purple.

Markaza narrowed her eyes. "Watch me."

"I'm calling your father!"

"Fine by me. Tell him I said hi." She spun around and stalked to the door. Her "minor" alterations of the dress included removing the fabric above the sweetheart neckline, lifting the hem to a scandalous height, and having large cutouts made up the back in the shape of hearts. It still flared when she spun around, and she laughed when she thought about how it would look on the dance floor.

People poured through the door and mingled around the stage, laughing and talking with one another.

Markaza made the rounds a number of times and was just getting her groove on when the bell rang again. "Mom! Could you get that?"

When the doorbell chimed a second and third time, she huffed and stopped shaking her butt. "I'll be right back. Sorry."

The guy she'd been dancing with shrugged and turned around.

She hoofed it to the door, cursing under her breath the whole way. When she opened it, her first thought was that a hot, cop stripper had been hired by someone. Throwing her head back, she laughed. "Come on in, hot stuff."

He lifted an eyebrow. "Mrs. Pamela Turner?"

"No way. You're looking for Ms. Markaza Turner. It's *my* birthday. Pamela's my mom."

Taking off his hat, he stepped through the door. "Is your mother at home, Miss?"

Markaza leaned in. "It's okay. She's here, but she won't mind me having a stripper. Not much she can do about it anyway, right? You're already here!" She backed up and checked him out. *Not bad at all.*

"Ma'am, there must be some confusion. I'm officer Deveaux with the NYPD, and I'm here to speak to Mrs. Pamela Turner."

"Suuuure you are! Right this way," she said, gesturing with a sweep of her arm.

When he stepped around her, she dropped her left hand and gave his butt cheek a squeeze.

He jumped and spun around. "That's quite enough, young lady. I'm here to see your mother. If you don't get her right now, I'll place you under arrest for assaulting a police officer."

Her eyes widened. "Wait… You're a *real* cop?"

"That's what I've been trying to tell you."

A vision she had two days prior assaulted her mind as she stared at him. In that moment, she knew why he'd come. Her father was dead. She began backing up, shaking her head, knowing any moment the officer was going to affirm her biggest fear.

When her vision came, she'd walked on eggshells the next day, waiting to hear news of her dad's death. It didn't happen, and she relaxed, thinking it was another miss. What he'd been doing in the car was nothing short of disgusting; and she'd had to witness the whole thing.

Deveaux's hand shot out, and he grabbed her wrist. "Don't run away. I need to talk to you, too."

Pamela rounded the corner. "What's all this?"

His eyes never left Markaza's as he talked. "I need to speak with you and your daughter, ma'am. Is there somewhere we can go and have a private conversation?"

"Of course. Follow me."

They made their way to the sitting room, and Officer Deveaux closed the doors.

"What is it you wanted to tell me?" Mom asked.

"Please, sit down."

Markaza's mother had a death grip on her daughter's arm. They moved in tandem to the couch and lowered themselves to the cushions.

"Now, what is it, Officer Deveaux? As you can see, my daughter is in the middle of her sweet sixteen party." Despite the shaking in Pamela's hands, she managed to keep her voice pretty steady.

He nodded. "I realize that. And I'm sorry I have to be the bearer of bad news on her birthday." His eyes cast around the room before settling on the floor. "There was an accident. Your husband…"

Mom's eyes went wide, and her hand flew to her mouth. "Is he… okay?"

Deveaux shook his head. "No ma'am. I'm sorry to have to be the one to tell you this; but, he was in a vehicular collision and died instantly."

Her head moved up and down, and her lips pressed together. "I see. Was he alone?"

He scanned her face, and his eyes narrowed. "Are you okay, ma'am? Is there someone I can call for you?"

She shook her head. It began gently at first, but deteriorated into a violent whipping from side to side.

Markaza had taken it in without saying a word. When her mother began a tirade, Markaza grabbed the woman. "Mom?"

"No, no, no, no." It was all she was saying.

Turning to the officer, Markaza stood up and stuck out her hand to him. "Thank you for letting us know about my father. I'll take care of it from here."

He shook her hand and gave apologies about intruding on her birthday party.

She showed him to the door.

Before he walked out, he turned and snatched her wrist. "You're taking this awfully well. Why did you back away from me earlier?" His eyes bored holes into hers.

"I knew this day would come eventually. My father isn't a real straight shooter, Mr. Deveaux. Besides, I'm not fond of cops." Even as she said the words, she knew the officer wouldn't believe them.

He was looking at her like he knew her secret. "You looked like you recognized me."

Her heart sped up. "I was mistaken. You look like a boy I used to know."

With a tug, he pulled her closer. "Why don't I believe you?"

Suddenly, for no reason she could think of, she wanted to tell that man everything. From the first vision to the last and her whole life in between. She gasped. "I don't know."

His scent was overpowering, and her breath hitched in her throat.

"Are you psychic?" he whispered.

Because her brain was so addled by his closeness, she floundered for a reply that would sound conceivable. "Uh…"

A smile broke out on his face. "Somehow, I knew it. That explains a lot. Here's my card. I'll be in touch, Ms. Turner." He turned and walked away with a wave over his shoulder.

Markaza leaned against the doorframe, trying to catch her breath. Never had a male affected her the way that one had. Her eyes never left his form until he disappeared into the elevator.

Snapping back to reality, she remembered her mother and the state she was in when Markaza left.

She clacked back through the house to the sitting room.

No one was there.

Figuring her mom had gone back to the party, Markaza meandered through the rooms, searching.

Pamela was nowhere to be found.

Finally, Markaza decided to try the bedroom. She eased up to the door and knocked. "Mom? You in there?"

There was no response.

She wiggled the knob and found it locked. "Mom? You need to open up. Tell me what all that was about."

Just when she was about to give up and break up the party, a click sounded. She turned to find her mother standing in the doorway, eyes red-rimmed, hair mussed, and wearing a robe.

"Mom?" Markaza's stomach tightened.

"Come in."

She stepped through the door and sat on the edge of the bed. "You okay, Mom?"

Pamela joined her daughter and took her hand. "I never understood how horrible those visions must be for you. I'm so sorry, honey."

While Markaza was enjoying the apologies falling from her mother's mouth, they caused a terrible fear to wash over the girl. "Oh, no…"

Mom nodded. "I saw it all."

"Then you know?"

Her head moved more violently. "I can't believe he did this to me!" As she spoke, her voice rose to a shriek that turned into a high-pitched scream.

Markaza put her hands over her ears. "Mom! Stop!"

Pamela threw everything she could get her hands on, and the bedroom became a tornado of destruction.

"Please, Mom! Stop!" Her daughter backed toward the door while begging. A vase crashed into the wall near her head.

Mom wailed at the top of her lungs.

Markaza's eyes filled with tears as she witnessed the collapse of everything she held dear. Quietly, she opened the door and fled.

After sending the guests away with profuse thanks and apologies, she picked up the phone to call the funeral home and make arrangements for her father. They promised everything would be done expediently. She hung up and went to her room, where she threw herself on the bed and gave in to the tears she'd managed to hold back for so long.

***

A week later, she saw Officer Deveaux at the cemetery with the other mourners. Once the rites were done and her father was lowered into his grave, she headed straight for the sultry, handsome cop. "Fancy meeting you here."

"I wasn't sure I was welcome." Dressed in a plain black suit, he looked younger than he had in the apartment. He gave her a timid smile. "But I had to try."

Markaza's inner goddess twirled. "Why?"

"Because I had to see you again. You've intrigued me, Ms. Turner." When he lifted his eyes to hers, they were wide and soulful. "And you didn't call."

Her heart did a flip. *Damn, he's hot!* "And how did I do that, Mr. Deveaux?"

He moved closer to her and inhaled. "Your eyes, your lips, the way you stand, and everything else; including that remarkable ability I know you have."

She pushed him back a bit and smiled. "You do know I'm only sixteen, right?"

"I do."

An eyebrow worked its way into her hairline.

"I'm only nineteen."

"It's still illegal."

"Not after another two years. Besides, who says we can't be friends? That's not illegal. I can wait for more."

A laugh escaped her lips. "You're right. But a hunch tells me you want to be more than friends."

He gave her a smile that showed all his teeth. "Anyone who can grab a butt with as much skill as you do deserves to be chased after."

Her face filled with heat.

"Are you blushing, Ms. Turner?"

"Who? Me?" She feigned surprise.

"So? Whaddya say? Wanna be my friend?" His voice had turned low and husky.

"You know what? I think I do, Mr. Deveaux."

***

"And that began our whirlwind romance type relationship… thing. As you can see, it was something good out of something very bad." Markaza barked out a laugh. "My mom hasn't left her room since that day. Last time I was in there, I noticed she'd stuffed a bunch of pillows into my dad's clothes and had them propped up in the bed. She's really sick, but I can't get her to come out of there.

"I went to court, with Richard's help, and took control of the hotel away from her. Some days are better than others. Those are the ones where she's lucid and seems to have an idea of what's really going on." She dropped her head into her hands.

One by one, the girls came over and gave her a hug.

"That's horrible. I can't believe you see that kinda stuff," said Shelia.

"I see worse things than that. But, I still need to explain why I came looking for all of you. Our time is running out." Markaza took a deep breath. "It happened last year on the day I turned seventeen…"

CHAPTER FIVE

THE END
OF THE WORLD

Markaza sat up and grabbed for the phone. Checking the time, she turned the device on and dialed Richard.

His voice was gravely.

"I'm sorry. I thought you might've been up. Want me to let you go?"

"No, no. I'm up. What's wrong?"

"Today's my seventeenth birthday." She picked at the blanket covering her bed.

"Uh oh. Happy birthday? Did it happen again?"

"Thanks. I think. Yeah. Sort of." Her mind whirled as she contemplated dishing it all out or writing it off as insanity. Because he was quiet, she assumed he was waiting on her to elaborate. It wasn't going to happen.

"Sweetheart?"

"Hm?"

"Are you gonna tell me what the dream was about?" His voice was low and soothing.

"Quit pulling your cop shit on me. I'm not some criminal you have to keep calm." As soon as the words left her mouth, she put a hand up. "Shit. I'm sorry."

He chuckled, and the sound went right to her heart. "It's okay. So, if you didn't wanna tell me, why'd you call?"

"I, uh…" Not sure how to explain without sounding like a wimpy girl who just needed to hear the voice of someone who cared, she let it drop.

A yawning sound filled the receiver, and she found herself smiling. He groaned like he was having the best stretch of his life. "Okay, we won't talk about it. Wow. That kitty stretch felt good. What are you doing today? Big plans?"

Oh, yeah, I just have to gather a bunch of women before December 21, 2012, convince them to fight, and hope we can stop the world from being destroyed. But her mouth parroted her usual phrase. "No, not really. I just have some internet research to do." *Hacking is more like it.* Markaza slapped her palm to her forehead. There was no way she could tell him what she saw. It pulled a sigh from her, and she slumped back on the pillows.

"That sounds ominous," he said.

She chuffed. "You have no idea."

"Well, if you aren't gonna tell me why you woke me up at"—there was a noise like he was moving to check his clock—"holy hell! Five in the morning? Wow. Okay, I should get off the phone and go back to sleep."

Another huff left her lungs.

"Talk later?"

"No. I'll tell you what I saw. Promise not to think I'm crazy?"

His voice suddenly sounded much more alert. "Of course I promise. You aren't crazy. I've seen what you can do first hand. What you *are* is amazing."

She was glad he was on the other end of the phone and not looking her in the face, because she was positive she was bright red.

"I know you're blushing right now. Don't be so modest."

What was already warm became an inferno. "Stop that."

He let another chuckle out. "Enough lollygagging. Spill."

After a deep breath in and out, she began. "I saw our entire world burned, broken, and in chaos. You know all those doomsday folks who say the world's gonna end on twelve, twenty-one, twelve?"

"Yeah." It was barely a whisper.

"As you know, that's my eighteenth birthday."

Silence.

She waited a whole minute before speaking again. "Hello?"

"Yeah, I'm still here. Wow. Really?"

"Uh huh."

"So, how do we stop it?" he asked.

A huge smile broke out over her face when he said "we," but she stifled a laugh because she knew he was deadly serious. "I saw a group of five women with me. There was this horrible monster"—a shiver worked its way up her spine—"it was the biggest thing I've ever seen. Taller than most of the buildings around it. And we were in Central Park."

"Oh, shit."

"My sentiments exactly. But these girls could do things. One was throwing around red light, another was singing like she was trying to lure the beast to sleep, and still another seemed to be shielding the scene from anyone who might happen upon us. I just have one problem."

Gurgles from a coffee pot could be heard from his side, so loud they almost drowned his voice out. He yelled, "What's that?"

"I don't know who they are," she yelled back.

"Can you find them?"

"Maybe. I have a few methods."

All the echoes stopped, and he came through more clearly. "I've seen your methods. Think it'll work?"

"It has to."

"What'll you do once you have these girls together?"

Giving an eye roll, she threw an arm up to cover her face. "I guess I have to teach them to use their powers and then take them to war."

He blew air out. "You know, I can't think of a more able person than you. If anyone can pull this shit off…"

"I hope you're right."

"I am. If you need any kind of help or anything, let me know, okay?"

"All right."

"Markaza?"

"Yeah?"

"I'm serious. You can ask."

"I know. Thanks."

They hung up, and she got out of bed to make coffee of her own. None of the dreams since she was thirteen had been quite so vivid or scary, but she'd learned not to freak out at what she saw. There were too many ways things could be stopped if she had enough information.

Once the coffee was brewing, she sat down at her crystal ball and concentrated.

***

"And that's how I managed to find all of you. What we're up against, whatever that beast is, we won't win if we don't work together." Markaza sighed and sat back in her chair.

Tension in the room was so thick, the air tasted of raw emotion—bitter and tangy, with a hint of intermingled perfumes.

Melody asked, "How do we know anything will come out okay? We could fail, and the world could go to hell in a Johnny-jumper!"

Everyone looked at her in wide-eyed shock then doubled over with laughter.

"Did you just say to hell in a Johnny-jumper?" Bronya asked. "Who says that?"

"Oh my God. That's *funny*!" Coralie was bent in half, holding her stomach.

Even Melody had a grin on her beet-red face. She shrugged and shook her head. "Y'all are crazy."

"Okay, ladies!" Markaza clapped her hands. "Let's get to bed. We need to get started early tomorrow. Melody has her appointment with the doctor at eight, so we'll be heading out right after."

"For what?" Bronya asked.

Markaza smiled. "Training, of course." She picked up the baggies. "First, I want you three to have these." One was given to Shelia, one to Melody, and one to Coralie.

Melody fished out the necklace and put it on. "What's it for?"

"Those are for protection. So no one, and nothing, can turn your power back on you once you attack with it. I had a little help from a woman in New Orleans. She sold me the materials to make them, and she gave me some tips," Markaza answered, thinking about the bracelet with the bones on it.

Shelia and Coralie put their necklaces on, too.

"How do they work?" Coralie asked, holding the stone up to her nose and squinting.

"I don't know. I just know we'll understand how to use them when the time is right." Markaza directed her gaze at Bronya and Lily. "You both have yours already. Please, wear them from now on."

Bronya saluted. "Will do, boss!"

"Goodnight, ladies. I'll see you for practice in the morning. If you have a minute or two, read some of your book. It may help you prepare." Spinning around, Markaza went to her room, shut the door, and put her forehead against the wood. "I sure hope that voodoo woman knew her stuff."

CHAPTER SIX

POWER PLAYS

Markaza crept out of bed at six the next morning, careful not to wake the others. Stepping out of her clothes from the night before, she wiggled her legs into a pair of jeans, donned a comfy t-shirt, and stuck her feet into sandals before heading toward the door and the meeting with Nancy.

Closing the door with barely a click and pressing the button to call the elevator, Markaza stared down the hall at her mother's suite for a moment while waiting on her ride to arrive. A ding startled the girl out of her blank stare, and she gave a small chuff as she stepped on.

Nancy greeted Markaza in the lobby.

"Hey yourself. What did you wanna talk to me about concerning Mom?"

"Let's go in the office. I don't want the staff to hear."

She shrugged. "Lead the way."

Looking back as though to check they weren't being followed, Nancy stuck her key in the door and pushed it open. She ushered Markaza in, glanced left and right, and let the door close on its own before walking back to the desk and dropping into the chair.

Markaza shifted from foot to foot. "Is everything okay?" Her mind raced with the possibilities.

"Yes and no. Your mother's health is the same, but she's started painting on the walls of her apartment."

"Painting?"

Nancy nodded and pressed her lips together.

"Well? What's she painting?"

"Some kind of demon."

Markaza's blood ran cold, but she tried to maintain a straight face. "Is that all?"

"Is that *all*? Isn't that enough? She's scaring the only cleaning woman who dares to go in there!" Nancy lifted an eyebrow. "You know something."

"Why do you always think I know what's going on?" To drive the point home, Markaza threw her arms out to each side and widened her eyes.

Nancy smirked. "Because you always do."

She hit the nail on the head with that statement, and Markaza dropped her hands to her hips. "Okay, let's say I know something about something. What's the demon in the paintings doing?"

"I think you need to see them. I know you haven't been up there in a while"—Nancy took a deep breath—"but you really should make the time."

"Can't you just tell me?"

"I'm not sure you'd get the full effect."

"Is this why we're acting like James Bond with all the secrecy and assuming spies are following us?"

"Yes. If any of the other staff members find out what's on those walls, they might quit. We've managed to build a dynamite team at this hotel, and I don't want our competition stealing our employees. I also don't relish the thought of our employees running their mouths to other establishments about a crazy woman being locked in the penthouse."

Markaza sighed and dropped her hands. "Okay. But I don't have a lot of time. The others will wake up soon and wonder where I went."

Standing, Nancy nodded once and walked toward the door.

*****

Black paint was dried in hard drops where it had oozed down the walls. Markaza was riveted to the drawings; they were identical to the creature in her visions and depicted the team of young women perfectly.

"Those look like your friends," Nancy whispered.

"I never knew Mom could paint like this."

"Neither did I. The details really bring them to life, huh?"

As the images progressed around the room, they told a chilling tale of destruction and death. In one, the creature had a young lady in its hand. In the next, there were only five girls and a lot of blood. Markaza shuddered as she recalled the vision she'd had in Atlanta. *Mom must be seeing things. That explains a lot...*

Nancy poked Markaza in the shoulder. "Is all this stuff real?"

She nodded. "I've seen some of it. But this one"—she pointed to the largest, covering several feet of the wall—"is new. It isn't something I've seen before."

Appreciation for the cleaning lady's fear lodged in Markaza's stomach as she stared at the gruesome painting. Pieces of bodies lay in various places—including heads, which were done with such amazing detail she could see the bloodshot eyes—and the creature was tearing into a building right near the park. Bricks flew in every direction, children falling from the top floors. Policemen in full riot gear had their guns aimed at the head of the being. Her hand flew up and touched one of the officers. *Deveaux.* She snatched her hand back and turned to Nancy. "Have this painted over. Take all pens, pencils, and paint supplies out of this apartment. No matter how much she begs, don't give her anything else to draw with. Please."

Markaza turned to walk away, but stopped short of the door. "I can't tell you what all this is about, but trust me when I tell you I'm doing everything I can to change the future. If you have to, get the doctors to medicate her until this is over. I'll make it better after that."

"For how long?"

"Until my birthday."

Nancy gasped.

Pulling the door open, Markaza fled to the safety of her apartment. Once she was back in her room, she allowed herself a moment to catch her breath. That's when the tears began. Like a tidal wave of anguish, sadness rolled over her. She cried until she had no breath left. For her father, for her mother, and for the incredible weight of responsibility that had been laid on Markaza's seventeen-year-old shoulders, her tears flowed. Then, she slept.

***

A knock at the door pulled her out of her comatose state. She glanced at the clock before dragging herself back out of bed. What was really only an hour nap felt like days, and energy coursed through her body. When she opened the door, she couldn't help but smile at Lily.

Warmth radiated off her slim frame, making her as welcome a sight as sunshine on a cloudy day. Not to mention the blinding smile she wore.

"Good morning. What's up?" Markaza asked.

"We've been waiting on you. We're excited to get out and do some training! You coming?"

She nodded. "Be right there."

"Okay. Hurry up! Melody's back and we wanna go." Lily bounced down the hall. "Oh, and we already made coffee!"

Markaza chuckled, pushed her door shut, and stepped into the bathroom to brush her teeth.

Five minutes later, she was in the kitchen with the others.

"So, what's the plan for today?" Coralie asked. "I'm eager to learn how to use this weird guide thing."

"I can't wait to see what we can do. From the display we had when Shelia's aunt showed up, I think all our powers together are gonna be awesome." Bronya smirked. "If we can learn to control them, that is."

Markaza took a deep breath and pushed her hair out of her face. "I think we need to practice Melody and Lily in public, the rest of us are too obvious. Shelia's powers are strange, and I'm not sure if they'll work without her violin, but I think that's better tried inside—away from prying eyes." Lifting her cup, she took a long drink and let the warm liquid flow down her throat as a balm for her nerves. "That picture's still out there, too. We can't let anyone else have the chance to snap one. I'm still waiting for us to be on the front page of the newspaper or something."

Coralie put up a hand. "Wait. What?"

"Some dude tried to mug Lily. We just did what we needed to do," Bronya answered.

"Because they were out after dark, like I asked them not to be. I saw it coming. You guys have to be more careful. If the public finds out what we are, we're gonna end up in a facility with tubes in our brains." Markaza looked at each of the ladies in turn. "Promise me."

They lifted a hand. "We promise."

"Can we go now?" Melody squealed.

"Yeah." Markaza paused and turned her head to the side. "Hang on a sec." Straining her ears, she picked up the barest hint of a conversation. "Do any of you hear that?"

Silence filled the room as everyone stared at Markaza. She closed her eyes and quieted her breathing.

"You know she'll flip out if she catches us." Male. Sounded young.

A second male spoke. "How's she going to catch us?"

When the third voice came through, it was obviously a female. "Yeah, how?"

Back to the first one. "Rumor has it she can see through walls. Last time someone stole something, they ended up without a job, and no one in the city would hire them. They had to move out of the state!"

"Just put it in the car." Female.

Markaza opened her eyes. "We need to go to the parking garage. Ladies, your first mission just fell in your laps."

Shelia asked, "What did you hear?"

"Some folks are about to steal something from my hotel. Let's make sure they don't get away with it, shall we?"

"You mean you heard them talking all the way from the garage?" Bronya's eyebrow was up, and her mouth was turned down.

"Yeah, I guess I did," Markaza answered.

"Holy crap," Shelia said.

"Let's go!" Lily's eyes glinted.

Coralie grinned. "Nothing would surprise me at this point. We're awesome."

"So, Coralie, how should we proceed?" Markaza asked. She watched as the girl closed her eyes, and a smile worked its way onto her lips.

After a moment, Coralie laid out the plan.

***

Markaza and Bronya made their way toward the back corner of the lower parking deck where three cars were sitting with the trunks open. Two males and one female, all in hotel uniforms, were loading up paintings.

"Those little pricks! What the fuck do they think they're doing?" Anger swelled in Markaza's stomach as she watched the art from the storeroom disappear.

"Calm down. Let's see if Coralie was right."

Pushing down the rage, she clenched her jaw, hopeful the upcoming scene would be enough to bring some humor to an otherwise serious situation.

Lily sauntered out of the shadows, looking as beautiful as a woman could.

Both young men stopped what they were doing to stare.

She turned her eyes toward the boys, giving them a come-hither smile, and dropped her purse—the contents scattering over the ground. When she leaned down to retrieve her wallet, her dress lifted high enough to give them a good look at her legs, stopping short of flashing all her lady bits.

At once, they were on the move, heading toward her belongings.

Music filled the space as Melody's voice echoed through, and the scene shifted to depict the inside of an art studio. Lily glowed yellow.

From behind the pillar, Markaza could see Coralie move toward the stolen artwork still piled by the storeroom door.

On cue, Shelia developed from the shadows, dressed in artist's garb, and strode toward the young men. It wasn't long before the female employee came out to join her partners.

Shelia lifted a paintbrush and dabbed it on the pallet on her arm. "Now, you two, move to that couch and undress." Her voice had a strange timbre to it. She motioned to the young men, directing them to a chaise lounge that materialized nearby.

They moved as they were told, and began to strip down.

"You"—she pointed to the girl—"stand over there. Take off your clothes! Make it quick. I don't have all day. You agreed to this."

"Yes, I agreed." Her clothes dropped in layers until she was in nothing but a bra and panties.

Markaza stifled a laugh.

"My assistant will put you in position and make you more comfortable." Shelia's voice rang with authority as it vibrated through the air.

Lily's light flickered, and the scene wavered.

"No. Stay focused," Markaza whispered.

Like the girl heard the whispered words, she lifted her hands to her face and the false surroundings re-solidified.

On cue, Bronya rose and stepped from the shadows with a pair of handcuffs dangling from one finger. She approached the three thieves and proceeded to pass their arms around one another, cuffing them in a circle. They were in their underwear, hugging, unable to move.

Coralie moved the last of the paintings through the door and gave a low whistle, signaling the charade was done.

Markaza stepped from her hiding place.

Lily dropped her arms and was caught before she hit the floor by Bronya. She lifted Lily as if she weighed no more than a feather, and carried her away, Coralie close behind.

Shelia's orange light faded. "You remember nothing after trying to steal the paintings," she said.

As one, the three replied, "We were stealing the paintings."

"You'll tell the police what you were planning."

"We'll tell the police what we were planning."

Her glow dissipated, and she nodded at Markaza. "They're ready for you."

"Thanks. Go on up with the others. Deveaux is on his way. I'll do the explaining."

Shelia nodded and left.

THE MYSTIC

"Now, tell me, which one of you had the stupid idea of stealing from me?" Markaza demanded.

CHAPTER SEVEN

RICHARD DEVEAUX

Markaza's heart sped up when Richard stepped out of the car and smiled at her. It had been too long since she'd seen him, and all she wanted to do was run into his arms. But, as it had been from day one, she refrained. He was nothing if not law abiding, and he'd insisted they wait until she was eighteen for any kind of overly affectionate behavior.

It was the end of July, and she hadn't seen or talked to him since she began her crazy mission to collect the others back in January. A brief moment of wondering if he'd moved on since then was washed away when he approached and took her hand. Tingles shot up her arm and tickled her heart.

"I've missed you."

She felt her face get warm as his eyes moved over her. Mentally, she slapped herself. "I've missed you, too."

Their moment was interrupted by a screech from the young lady handcuffed to the two boys.

Richard turned and glared at them. He became all business. Head high, shoulders back, and notepad in hand. "What do we have here?"

Markaza filled him in about the attempted theft, he made an arrest, and the three thieves admitted everything. From the looks on their faces, none of what they said was intentional. It seemed their mouths were moving no matter how hard the youngsters fought. She hid a smile behind her hand as they were loaded into the police car.

Before Richard got in the driver's seat, he gave Markaza a smile. "Call me, okay? I'd like to know what you've been up to. Seven months is a long time."

She nodded and waved as he drove away.

***

Once she was in the elevator, she allowed herself to breathe fully. Things with Richard had been complicated, but her eighteenth birthday was right around the corner. Maybe they'd find a way to finally be together. Her virginity was intact, thanks to her status as a weirdo, and she couldn't think of a more deserving person to give it to. Perhaps. One day.

If they survived beyond the end of December.

A ding, signaling her arrival, startled her out of her thoughts.

Female voices echoed down the hallway. Markaza smiled and threw open the apartment door. "Ladies, *that* was amazing!"

Bronya lifted her mug. "I'll drink to that!"

Laughter burst forth from the others.

"What are you guys drinking?"

Lily answered, "Coffee."

"I couldn't think of a more perfect drink. Pour me one!"

"Markaza's back! Now will you tell us how you knew it would work?" Shelia asked Coralie.

"I saw all these blocks of text in my head. Some were gray, and some were green. When I followed the green ones, it formed a whole plan of attack and resolution," she answered.

Lily shoved a cup of coffee at Markaza, and she took a long drink before asking, "Do you remember what the gray ones said?"

Coralie shook her head. "That's the weird thing. Once I didn't choose that path, all the text blocks disappeared. I couldn't see them anymore. Even though I read the words, they didn't stay with me."

"Hmm…" Markaza drummed her fingers on the counter. "So, once you choose a path, that's the one we have to follow."

"I'm not sure. It's almost like it set the path for me and discarded all others."

"But what if there are two paths that'll lead to the same outcome?"

Coralie shrugged.

"We'll have to play around with it some more." Markaza panned her eyes over the others until her gaze landed on Shelia. "Did you know you could do that without your violin?"

"I… Well, yeah. Kind of."

"How?"

"I told you about Aunt Ivy's visit…" Shelia became interested in the hem of her shirt.

"Go on."

"I kind of convinced her to leave and not come back. I'm not sure how."

Markaza said, "So you have the same power I do."

Shelia shrugged. "I'm not sure. None of us know how all this works. I just know I can tell people to think things and they do."

"Anyone wanna be a guinea pig?"

Melody's hand went up.

"Perfect. Let's go to the living room. I wanna try something," Markaza said.

There were whoops of joy as the ladies made their way to the couches.

Melody stood in the middle of the circle with her hands on her hips. "What do you want me to do?"

"Just stand there," Markaza answered. "Shelia, come stand by me. Wow. That sounded like an '80s hit title, huh?"

"Because it kinda was," Bronya said.

Coralie sang, "Oh darlin', darlin' stand…"

Markaza grinned as the others joined in. She let them sing for a few moments before interrupting. "Okay, okay. That's enough. Let's get to the fun part."

In an instant, the room fell silent.

"Now, Shelia, I want you to focus your power toward Melody. Convince her she needs to go to the bathroom."

Giggles.

"Shh! This is serious, guys." Markaza took a deep breath. "Just focus."

Shelia closed her eyes, put her palms to her thighs, and tapped a forefinger on her skin.

Orange lights spun around her legs, getting brighter and moving faster until they blurred and absorbed into her. She opened her eyes and spoke. "Melody." Vibrations from the words rolled through the room, visibly passing over everyone, ruffling their hair like a breeze over a wheat field. But Shelia's breath of wind contained power that collided with the center of Markaza's body, making her knees go weak.

Melody shifted her stance, and her shoulders dropped. She replied, "Yes. I hear you." Rather than the singsong timbre her voice usually had, it fell into a monotone when she spoke.

"You need to go to the bathroom. It's so urgent, you're afraid you won't make it. There isn't time to do anything else. Run."

Markaza shuddered as the speech flowed out over the room again.

Face contorted with pain, Melody let out a squeak and ran for the bathroom.

Shelia's orange glow faded, and she smiled. "Well? How'd I do?"

"That was incredible," Markaza answered. "I can make suggestions to people, and they tend to do what I say, but that was stronger than anything I've put out there."

"You can do what?" Bronya asked.

Markaza felt her face get warm. "I can control people by changing their thought process. It's not exactly what Shelia can do, but it's pretty close."

"Did you ever use that crap on me?"

"No. I didn't need to. I used it on Doctor Kurt when I needed him to let Melody out of the hospital."

"You used what on my doctor?" Melody was standing in the hallway, her eyes wide.

"It was the only way they'd let you leave. You weren't okay by the time we needed you to leave, but I knew we could help you here as much as they could there."

"What does that mean? I wasn't doing well?" Tears appeared as glistening drops yet to spill over the dam of her lids.

Markaza rushed over. "You were doing great! I just knew you were still too thin to be released and too fragile mentally to see yourself as you were. Lily helped me out with a little of her oculus charm, and we convinced the good doctor to let you go sooner than he would've. I have the staff here to take care of you, and the five of us have been helping where we could." She took Melody's hands. "Now, you look a lot healthier, and you've been improving by the day. I know you still think about it. You probably always will. But we're here to help you get through it all."

A face that betrayed the feelings of uncertainty lifted two glistening eyes. "You mean it?"

Everyone else joined in a group hug.

Bronya squeezed them all together and lifted them off the floor. "We love ya, kid! You're one of us now. We'll watch out for you forever."

Markaza nodded. "She's exactly right."

Melody smiled and looked around the group, her eyes settling on each young woman for a moment before moving on. "I love y'all."

"We love you, too!" It was a chorus of answers, overlapping with the same words.

In the midst of the laughter, the doorbell rang.

Markaza pried herself loose to answer. On the other side of the peephole stood detective Richard Deveaux.

Her breath hitched, and her heart fluttered like a hummingbird on speed. She opened the door and stepped into the hall, sealing the opening with a click. When she turned, she was inches from Richard's face.

He lifted a hand and put his palm to her cheek.

Nuzzling his warm flesh with her own, she looked up at him and felt her knees get weak.

A smoldering gaze met her own. Eyes any player would kill for raked over her body before coming back to lock on to their prey. And prey she was. Caught in the embrace of a lean predator.

"Hi," he whispered.

"What's all this?" Confusion ricochet through her, causing her heart and stomach to weld together in the ache of what she was sure would be loss in a moment. He'd never touched her like that, and she was terrified of what he'd do to her soul if he kept going the way he was.

"I got back to the station and couldn't stop thinking about you. It's been so long. I was worried I'd lost you." From passion to underlying anger, his features shifted. "Why'd you change your number? There was no way for me to make sure you were okay. Didn't you know how worried I'd be?"

Guilt tripped its way down Markaza's spine, and she sagged. "It was selfish of me." She gave his palm another sniff before pushing it away. "I needed to be alone so I could focus. There wasn't time to explain." Tears threatened, but she forced herself to calm down. "Besides, I knew you'd want to come with me or would've followed me."

"You knew right."

"But you being there would've ruined everything. I needed to do it on my own. There was no way these women would've trusted me if I'd shown up with a man. Most of them have been hurt in some way by men. I just couldn't." She didn't add *as much as I wanted to.*

"So you decided not to talk to me at all? To tell me nothing?"

"I know." She sighed. "It was stupid and immature."

"Look, I'm not mad. I mean, I was at first, but I'm not anymore…" Richard rubbed his hand over his face. "Can we go inside for a few minutes?" He closed the distance between them. "Please?"

"There are five other women in there."

"I know. I want… No, I need to be alone with you for a minute. Out here"—he gestured to the hallway—"there are cameras."

Heat rushed to her cheeks, down her neck, and made a beeline for her crotch. If he was saying what she thought he was…

Her hesitation must've made him think she was afraid because he lifted his brows and grabbed her hands. "I promise, it's not what you think. There's a place inside of me that just needs to be close with you for a moment."

She opened the door and gestured. "After you, Detective Deveaux."

He waved to the women sitting at the table as he passed, eliciting catcalls, whistles, and exclamations that made Markaza blush.

Pulling him down the hall, she led him to her room before shutting and locking the door.

He was on her before the sound of the click faded, pressing her back to the wood. His lips caressed her neck, tickled her ear, and touched her closed eyelids before making a path back to her mouth.

No breath would enter her body as she waited for her fantasy from the previous year and a half to come true. Then, soft tickles, like a million butterflies tap dancing on the petals of flowers, were upon her lips. All the air was stolen from the room, for no matter how she gasped, she still couldn't fill her eager lungs. Her heart raced, pounding the blood through her body, drowning out all other sounds.

It was the most amazing thing she'd ever experienced, and she wanted more.

"Make love to me," she whispered.

He groaned and leaned against her, pressing his face into her neck, each breath rough on her neck. "Don't ask me to do that."

"Why?"

"Because you know I can't. You're not old enough, and I…"

She waited, but he didn't continue. "You're what?"

"I'm a police officer. I uphold the law; I don't break it."

"I know." It was all she could manage as her heart deflated like a spent pufferfish. As the passion ebbed away, it was replaced by fury and confusion. *He has some damned nerve!* She pushed him back and crossed her arms over her chest. "What the hell was all this, then?"

"I'm… sorry."

"Sorry? Is that all I get?"

"No. Please, let me explain."

"Okay. I'm waiting." Mentally, she berated her temper for taking over and letting her act like a spoiled brat. But he was playing with her emotions, and she didn't like it one bit.

"When you left, I kept waiting for you to call, text... I don't know... something. But you never did. Every day I sat here, thinking I'd lost you. Scared that you'd died or were hurt somewhere and I'd never know. I've never had a regret in my life, but I did when I thought of how many opportunities I'd had to kiss you, to *show* you how I felt about you inside, and never did. That would've stayed with me until the day I died." He spun around and grabbed her shoulders, giving her a gentle shake. "Markaza, I love you. If I'd never seen you again, knowing that you didn't know how I felt would've haunted my every waking moment." Then, his lips were on hers again, and her anger drained away as she allowed herself to feel the love pouring into her and understand the agony she'd caused.

Tears of joy and sorrow intermingled on her cheeks. In that moment, she knew she'd give her life to save his.

Chapter Eight

Earthquakes

Two months later, Richard was still dropping by nearly every day after work to spend time with Markaza. After talking to the girls for a little while, he and Markaza would go to her room and kiss, cuddle, and talk before he'd leave and she'd emerge looking disheveled.

One evening, after he'd left, Lily approached her mentor. "You've gotta tell him."

Alarm bells sounded in Markaza's head. "Tell him what?"

"About us."

"No way. No, no, no."

"What if he finds out?"

"He won't." Markaza choked on the lie. Richard already know what the girls could do—in theory. She coughed.

Lily curled her lip. "He almost caught me last week, remember? I had my real face on."

"We'll just have to be more careful about when we use our gifts." Telling Richard how the extent of their powers made them all some kind of superhero crazies was last on Markaza's "wish to do this year or ever" list. He'd think they were all nuts.

"He already knows you can see the future. Trust him, huh?"

"Says the girl who ran away from the only man she's looked at for more than a minute in the last year." Markaza cringed even as she said the words. She didn't feel like being lectured, and her mouth lost its filter for a moment.

"Ouch."

"Shit. I'm sorry." Before Lily could turn away, Markaza wrapped her arms around the girl and pulled her in for a hug. "My mouth runs on autopilot sometimes. I really didn't mean that. Totally uncalled for."

They stayed that way until Lily returned the embrace.

Only then would Markaza let go. "You're right. I need to tell him. Just let me do it in my own time, okay?" She fought internally about how she wanted to show him. Having him stumble on one of the girls practicing wouldn't go over well.

Lily nodded and smiled. "Let's go get something to eat. I'm—"

Around them, the walls began to move and the floor shook like the Earth was being knocked around on its axis.

Everyone screamed as glasses toppled on the table and spilled, windows rattled, and the world swayed.

"What the hell's going on?" Bronya yelled.

Markaza passed out.

Claws on the end of long, twisted, black fingers rake the ground, creating gouges two feet wide and three feet deep.

"I'm coming…"

Shaking brought her out of the vision. Lily had hold of her friend's shoulders and was in her face asking if she was okay. Everyone else was gathered around, their faces white.

"Yeah, yeah. I'm fine. Back up, would you?" Markaza sat for a moment. "Guys, I think it's time I told you the rest of the story."

Coralie and Shelia exchanged a glance Markaza didn't miss.

"Let's eat dinner, find out what the fuck that shaking was, and then I'll talk."

Melody was nominated to be the one to order, and the rest of the ladies gathered around the television where the news was blaring.

"It's confirmed. An earthquake measuring five point eight on the Richter scale has hit the Eastern United States. While it was centered in Portland, Maine, tremors were felt as far south as Georgia. We're going to Nick Wall, our reporter in the field. Nick?"

"I'm here with Hatty Keller, a resident of—"

Markaza flipped the television off.

No one spoke.

Thoughts raced through her head then fell out of her mouth. "If the creature is coming up in Central Park, why in God's name was the earthquake in Maine? What if I'm wrong and the thing isn't coming up here? But, no, I saw the police tape. We drove by there. It was obvious. Can it really have that broad of an impact? What if we're already too late? What if I missed the date? Got it wrong…"

Shelia touched Markaza's arm. "What are you talking about? Does this have anything to do with the hole we saw?"

"Yes."

Their doorbell rang, and a bellhop rolled in a cart full of food.

Markaza's mouth watered when the smell of steak and peppers flooded her nose. "Thanks, Geoff!"

He waved and gave her a little bow before exiting without a sound.

"Let's eat!"

Everyone avoided topics of earthquakes and monsters while they consumed dinner. Melody had done an excellent job ordering, and there were mountains of potatoes, salad, steak, slaw, and fries. She actually ate a little bit of everything.

Markaza sat back in her chair, smiled, and groaned. "I'm soooo full. Miserable."

"Me, too!" Bronya added.

"I think we should put off the discussion a little longer while we have after dinner coffee. Then I'll be ready to talk," Markaza said.

"Okay, but you're so spilling it *all* after," Bronya said.

"Deal."

Again, no one talked about anything but food, fashion, and who the hottest guys in movies were until the coffee ran out and Markaza was forced to face the music.

All eyes turned toward her.

"Okay, okay. Let's go sit."

They adjourned to the living room and made themselves comfortable.

Markaza plopped down in her chair and put her head in her hands. "I've been putting this off because I was afraid once you found out what you're expected to kill, destroy, whatever, you'd run."

Bronya growled. "Whatever it is, we're here. It'll take more than some horrific creature to get rid of us."

"It's not just a horror. I think, whatever it is, it's here to destroy every human on the planet. Something is happening in the world that's feeding this thing. It's a creature of some kind."

Melody's voice had a light tremor. "What do you mean, creature?"

"This thing's bigger than the tallest building in New York. Whatever it has in its fangs singes the grass in my visions; we have to assume the venom is acidic. Eyes that'll pierce you to your very soul glow red in a face that's pinched and leathery. Claws that could rip a Humvee in half without effort are attached to the thing's fingers. If you can call them fingers."

Markaza took a deep breath. "But the skin. It looks like all the trash in the city fell into a giant tar pit and fused together. Its voice is deep and rumbles with power like I've never encountered. Shelia's comes close, but she doesn't use her ability often. I think that's why it's not as strong. When you hear the creature speak, it rattles every bone in your body. You fill up with rage and loathing.

"It's bad, ladies. This thing has appeared to me so many times, I could draw enough detail to fry your pigtails." Visions of the paintings on her mother's apartment walls made their way into Markaza's head.

Nancy had taken care of it, even going so far as to relocate the cleaning woman with a handsome bonus if she promised not to talk to anyone about what she saw.

But the images had been very real.

"When was the last time, before today, that you had a vision?" Coralie asked.

"A month ago. Remember when we were in the restaurant downstairs and I passed out in my food?"

She nodded.

"Then. It was bad. Blood was everywhere." Markaza shoved her hands under her thighs to stop the shaking. "I think my mom's seeing it, too."

"Your mom?" Melody asked, her voice rising.

Markaza nodded. "Unless the doctor medicates her very heavily. She was painting stuff on the walls. There were some scenes there I'd never had visions of."

Melody gasped. "Is she okay?"

"Honestly, I don't know. I mean, I'm worried about her and all, but between Richard telling me he loves me and—"

"Awwwwwwww!" Lily squealed and clapped her hands together.

"And everything that's been going on with our training." Markaza lifted her lip at the endearment from her friend and shot her a look to keep her quiet. "I haven't had time."

"That's bullshit. She's your fucking mother." Coralie stood up, threw the pillow she'd been clutching at the couch, and stomped off.

"What's her problem?"

Shelia spoke softly. "Her parents ran off, remember? Like they didn't have *time* for her. They just cast her aside like she was nothing."

"I'm not giving up on my mom. I just need time to get things under control before I deal with her."

"And I'm sure Coralie spent a lot of time waiting for her parents to work out their shit so they could come back for her, too. Sorry. It probably hit a nerve. I'm gonna go check on her."

Markaza's stomach dropped. She hadn't intended to sound so callous, but her mother was safer where she was until everything blew over.

Everyone whispered between themselves until Shelia and Coralie re-appeared.

"Coralie, I—"

She held up a hand. "Don't. I have one more thing to say to you before I drop it."

"Okay."

"What if you never see her again? What if these are the last few weeks of your life, and you *never see your mother again*? What then? Will you be happy you kept her medicated and 'safe,' or will you wish you'd spent just five minutes trying to understand her anguish, fear, and confusion? That's all." Mouth pressed into a grim line, she made her way back to the couch and plopped down.

Markaza stared at the floor for a long moment before she spoke. "I understand where you're coming from. I'll think about it. Okay?"

Coralie nodded.

"When you call up the fight with this 'thing' in your head, is anything green?"

"I haven't tried."

"We need to focus on that soon. I'm exhausted, guys. Let's get some sleep." Markaza stood up and stretched. "Sorry to tell you horror stories before bed." She spun around and walked out.

Once she was back in the safety of her room, she curled her legs under her on the bed and pulled out the book they all had a copy of. Her fingers caressed the cover, and she flipped it open to the middle. There, wedged in between a couple of pages, was a printed photo of the huge scene her mother had painted. Markaza pulled it out and held it in her hands, studying it.

"This can't happen."

Hours later, she fell asleep with the photo clutched between her fingers, tears drying on her cheeks.

CHAPTER NINE

RETAIL THERAPY

A boom that shook the whole apartment jerked Markaza from her sleep and had her scrambling for the door. She yanked it open in time to see Melody fly past in her nightgown.

"What the hell was that?" Markaza screamed.

Laughter echoed down the hall.

She raced to the living room and screeched to a halt. Their couch was obliterated. Stuffing, pieces of wood, and chunks of fabric were everywhere.

"I see nothing funny about this."

Bronya's face was red, and she was gasping for air. "You should've seen it! I was trying to lift the couch so Lily could vacuum under it, and it just exploded." Another gasp. "It was contained. No one got hurt."

"No? I almost broke my face getting out of bed! That's not funny! How'd you lose control like that?"

There was no response but laughter.

"Shut. The. Fuck. Up. Now." Markaza's voice was low, and her fingernails were cutting into her palms. Inside, she was boiling. It was bad enough the couch had been reduced to kindling, but they were laughing about it? Not only would they need a new living room set, someone could've heard.

With a look like a chastised child, Bronya sobered and crossed her arms. "I don't know what happened. One minute it was in the air, the next…" She gestured to the mess.

Markaza paced so she wouldn't commit murder. "We're going stir-crazy being cooped up in here." She was mumbling to herself, but the others appeared to have heard.

Everyone nodded.

A split decision was made. "Okay, forget about the couch. I'll call Nancy, tell her to let anyone who calls know there's construction going on up here, and ask her to send a cleaning crew for the mess. Let's get outside. I need some air, and I think a little retail therapy would do us all some good." A smile took over her face. "Besides, we need a new couch."

Cheers broke out amongst the other women, and Lily started talking about the latest fashions with anyone who'd listen. It was as if a rainbow had shown up on a cloudy afternoon.

By the enthusiasm in the room, Markaza assumed the other ladies had been feeling restless for a while and were too nervous to bring it up. Their elation solidified the idea as a great one, and she skipped back to her room to get dressed. Truth be told, she was looking forward to getting out of the building as much as the others.

A quick shower and a touch of makeup later, she was ready to go. As she stared in the mirror, she decided another tattoo session was in order. There was something provocative about calf tattoos, and she'd had a picture of one she'd wanted to get for a while. She dug around in her nightstand, retrieved the photo, folded it, and tucked it in the pocket of her jeans before going back down the hall to the kitchen.

Everyone was there except Lily.

Shelia grinned and rolled her eyes. "She's still making herself fabulous."

When Lily finally emerged, half an hour later, she had on a pair of black shortalls with pink pockets, a white tank top, and black and pink high-heeled sandals with a butterfly pattern woven into the laces that covered her calves and tied at her knees. On her arm was a white Prada bag.

"When did you go shopping?" Markaza asked.

Lily shrugged. "Online."

Bronya let out a wolf whistle the other women repeated.

"Aren't you a hot mama?" Coralie teased.

"Hell yes I am," Lily responded. "Are you all ready?"

A chorus of yeses were given in response, and she led the way to the door.

Markaza picked up her phone and dialed the front desk as she followed everyone out. "Nancy? We're gonna need the limo. Oh, and if anyone asks, that boom this morning was our construction crew dropping equipment." She chuckled. "No, but we do have a bit of a mess up here."

By the time they reached the lobby, Johanna was lounging by the desk, waiting. She gave a wave and bounced over to them. "Long time no see, ladies. I thought you guys had fallen off the planet or something." Her cheery tone was punctuated by a perfect smile. "I was starting to feel bad being on the payroll around here. Felt like a waste of space."

"You, my dear, are never a waste of space." Markaza gave the woman a hug.

"Where we going today?"

"We're in need of a little retail therapy."

Johanna grinned. "Bloomingdale's, here we come!"

Lily and Shelia raced to the front door, squealing all the way. Bronya, Melody, and Coralie weren't far behind.

Markaza and Johanna brought up the rear.

"Wow. They're happy to be going out," she said.

"I've had them cooped up in that apartment for over a month. We all need some exercise outside the building. I think I need social interaction with greedy sales people, too." Markaza smirked.

"Are we gonna play the 'suck up to me because I own half of New York City's wealth' game today?"

"Hell to the *yes*. Call them. Let them know we're coming. This will be a day these girls will never forget. Tell them I want no less than ten stylists on hand."

Johanna winked. "You got it, boss."

When they got to the car, she opened the door with a flourish and bowed. "Your majesties."

Lily stuck her nose in the air, flipped her hands up, and sauntered past like the royalty she'd been addressed as.

Shelia giggled and crept past with her head down, and the other ladies piled in behind.

Once Johanna was in the front seat, she started the car, put on her sunglasses, and turned around. "You guys wanna see something neat?"

Coralie was the one who answered. "Yes! Not sure what you can show me in this burg that I haven't already seen, but I'm game."

"Perfect. Hold on to your hats, girls. You're about to *taste* New York."

Their car accelerated from the curb so fast, it elicited squeals from the backseat.

In a moment, the privacy glass went up.

"Is she okay up there?" Shelia whispered.

Markaza grinned. "Yes, she is. We've worked out a little surprise for you girls. I'm not sure where she's taking us right now, but you're gonna love what we have in store for you in a little while. Johanna's full of revelations. Sit back, relax, and take it all in."

Though Shelia sat back, she kept her eyebrows knit together—a sure sign she wasn't convinced.

Letting out a whoosh of air, Markaza closed her eyes and put her head back. Their car slowed sooner than she thought it should, and she snapped to attention. They were turning onto Avenue C.

A block later, and they pulled over.

Johanna dropped the privacy glass, said she'd be right back, and bolted to the front door of a place called Ninth Street Espresso.

Everyone in the car whispered about what could be going on. Before conclusions could be reached, Johanna reappeared. She was holding the door for two waiters carrying silver trays with porcelain cups and plates balanced on top. Once the guys were outside, she raced ahead and opened the back door of the car.

Lattes with pretty designs in the froth and slivers of cheesecake with heart shaped cherries drizzled over top were passed to the occupants. Sighs of pleasure followed.

Markaza caught a wink from Johanna before the door was shut, the waiters were tipped, and the car was put back into action.

Traffic was abysmal, and it took two hours to get to Bloomingdale's.

Conversation was all that flowed, and the girls chattered about everything known to God and man.

As the limo was pulling up to the doors of the store, everyone but Coralie had their faces pressed to the glass so they could look up at the building. A throng of people had gathered around a red carpet leading to the entrance—probably waiting on some big-name starlet to get out.

Lily was the first to exit. Tourists with cameras snapped photos of her as she posed and blew kisses.

Coralie went next. A couple of people who must've been New York natives pointed. Her name was called, but she moved on.

When Melody got out, there were cheers from the crowd.

Bronya glanced at Shelia. "Do you feel a little outta place?"

"Yeah…"

"Come on, ladies. Walk with me!" They were dragged from the car by Markaza. She walked the carpet like she had many times before, one hand on each of her friends.

Once the show was over, the young women were assaulted by sales people with perfect teeth, pristine clothing, and hair that had been sprayed to a marble-like state. Each woman was being fussed over by at least two people.

Johanna bowed, blew a kiss to the ladies, shut the door, and leaned against the car to wait.

"Isn't she coming in?" Shelia asked.

"No. She gets paid a lot of money to stand there and look pretty."

At her quizzical look, Markaza laughed, grabbed Shelia's hand, and pulled her along behind the staff members.

All day was spent shopping. New outfits, hairdos, swim-suits, manicures, makeup, and furniture for the living room were purchased.

Halfway through the fun, Markaza slipped out the door, got into a car with a petite blonde, and rode away. She didn't return for three hours. When she did, only one person seemed to have noticed her absence.

"Where'd you go?" Shelia asked.

Markaza reached over, pulled the sleeve of her t-shirt up, and peeled back a bandage on her arm to reveal a floral tattoo with angry, red skin around it. She wiggled her eyebrows. "I was gonna do something on my calf, but I didn't have time. Like it?"

"Ooooooh, that's gorgeous!"

"Thanks. I needed some pretty. Speaking of… You look amazing!"

Shelia's hair had been trimmed to frame her face, and she was wearing light makeup that just accentuated her features. When she blushed, the rosy glow added to the allure. "Thank you."

Markaza threw her arm around her friend's shoulders. "Where are the others?"

Shelia chuckled. "You're gonna laugh."

"Try me."

"They're in a mud bath in the spa."

"Oh my…" Markaza pressed her lips together. "How come you aren't in there with them?"

"It's not my scene."

"Not comfortable taking your clothes off yet?"

"No. I've been discussing it with my doctor. He says it's because of what Melvin did to me, but I'm not sure. I think it's because I don't like the way I look." Shelia's face turned red.

"Look?"

"Yeah. All this weight I'm carrying around."

Markaza held the girl at arm's length and looked her over. She had a few extra pounds, but they made her hips more seductive and round. "Your uncle was a fucktwad. Big time. Don't let him ruin the rest of your life like he has the last thirteen years. You're beautiful, voluptuous, and sexy. Don't you ever forget it."

"What if I don't want to be those things?"

"Huh?"

"It wasn't by accident that I gained so much weight. I thought… Well, if I were ugly…"

"I know. You told me. But nothing you can do on the outside can hide the beautiful person in here." Markaza put a finger on Shelia's chest near her heart. "That's what your uncle was after, and that's the one thing he never got. It's also the one thing he can never take from you. Do you understand what I'm saying?"

Shelia nodded.

"Good. Now, dry your eyes, and let's go get dirty!"

CHAPTER TEN

POSSESSION AND PERMEATION

Once the girls returned to the suite, they set about putting away the things they'd bought, making coffee, and chatting about nothing and everything all at once.

A knock on the door silenced them.

Markaza mumbled, "Wonder who that could be? Too soon for the furniture delivery." When she opened the door, she was surprised to find Nancy standing there, wringing her hands and glancing up and down the hall with red-rimmed eyes. "Nancy? You okay?"

Rather than speak, she shook her head and pressed her lips together.

"What happened?" Markaza asked, pulling the woman into the apartment and shutting the door.

Nancy's tears escaped, and hiccups punctuated her speech. "It's… Well… You see, your… She's gone and done it now!" Her hands flew to her face as the sobs flowed out.

All the young ladies raced to her side and made a circle of arms around her.

Shelia hummed under her breath, sending a blanket of calm to swaddle them.

After a moment, Nancy dropped her hands, took a deep breath, and released. "It's okay. Thank you, girls. I need to speak with Markaza alone for a moment." She gave a half smile, but her hands had stopped visibly trembling.

Markaza whispered a thanks to Shelia, and the girl continued to hum quietly as she and the others scattered throughout the space, leaving Nancy and Markaza as alone as they could be. "What happened?" Markaza asked.

"Your mother has taken the new cleaning woman hostage and won't release her until you make an appearance."

"What!" Her mind went bananas with the possible reasons her mother would go that far 'round the circus tent. There were no viable options that came to mind. "Why?" Markaza finally asked.

Nancy leaned in close and whispered, "I don't know. She didn't sound like herself."

Markaza lifted an eyebrow.

"I can only describe it as an oily, demonic voice. It was her, but not her."

Dry mouth assaulted her.

"I don't think this is something we'll be able to cover up. I had to give the last maid a huge bonus and find her a new job so she'd keep her mouth shut about the murals." Nancy twisted her hands together. "You don't think… Is this woman in danger? Real danger?"

Reaching around the worried woman, Markaza opened the door. "I don't know. Meet me there in five minutes."

Without waiting for an answer, she pushed the door shut and spun around. "Girls!"

They all ran to her, questions flying a light-year a second.

"Stop!"

Silence.

"I need you to come with me. It seems Pamela isn't doing very well."

Shelia glanced around. "What's going on with your mom?"

"She's taken a hostage—a maid. Nancy said the voice coming out of Pamela's mouth was hers, but it sounded demonic. I think we have a classic case of possession here, though I won't be sure until I see her." Markaza took a deep breath and slowly let it out. "It's him. I know it is." She grimaced. "Anyone know how to do an exorcism?"

"Are you kidding?" Bronya's face was tight, and her eyes were wide.

"I'm afraid not. Maybe he'll leave on his own, but I think I'm gonna have to go down there. Which one of you wants to go with me?"

All five hands shot into the air.

Markaza smiled. "Okay then. Let's go. Please try to keep in mind this is my mother." Steeling her nerves, she led them down the hall to her mother's suite, where Nancy was waiting outside the door.

At her questioning look, Markaza shook her head. "Don't ask. They need to see this. I think it's part of something much, much bigger."

Nancy nodded, stuck the key in the door, unlocked it, and pushed it open.

"Aren't you coming?" Markaza asked.

"No. I've seen her. I'll wait here."

The young women filed into the suite, Lily pausing to hug Nancy. "It'll be okay. We'll be right back."

Carefully, they tiptoed across the wood floors until they got to Pamela's room. Markaza put her ear to the door.

A stream of rapid Spanish in a female tone could be heard. Then, the sound of skin being slapped. Markaza jerked her head back. *Did Mom just hit the cleaning lady?*

Bronya's hands were glowing, and she put one on the closed door. "Just say the word, and this thing's coming off the hinges."

Everyone took cover, and Markaza nodded.

Splinters of wood flew in every direction as the door exploded. Pieces ricocheted off the wall of red light around Bronya before they could make contact.

A pretty Spanish girl sat on the end of the bed, a look of horror on her face.

Markaza rushed in and pointed a finger at the young woman. "Are you okay?"

She nodded. "Jes. I am okay." In a more confrontational tone, she asked, "Are ju okay?"

Pamela was laughing and holding her sides. "What in the world is going on? Exploding doors? Really, Markaza, your flare for the dramatic is touching."

A forest surrounded them, complete with Spanish moss and a little stream gurgling by. Markaza and her mother were the only two there.

Golden light glinted in Pamela's eyes and her voice changed. "What'sss thisss? Where did she go?"

Tingles erupted between Markaza's thighs, and she clenched the muscles to keep from peeing her pants. It was the creature's voice, and it was so much worse than it had been in her visions. Fear bounced through her limbs, and she struggled to keep her knees from buckling as a feeling of hopelessness washed over her. Praying her voice didn't tremor, she lifted her chin and drew anger from the depths of her soul. "There you are. What the fuck are you doing to my mother?"

"You mean thissss? The mother you hate?" The creature who was Pamela spun in a circle and let out a wicked laugh. "Why do you care?"

Their surroundings flickered and disappeared. They were back in the bedroom.

Five glowing women surrounded Markaza, bathing the room in a rainbow of brilliance.

Bronya, red and angry, stepped forward. "What is it you want?"

Pamela's features flickered, and the image of the beast was clear for a fraction of a millisecond. It roared, "To destroy you!" Vases—priceless artifacts from a collection long thought lost to most collectors—flew at the group from around the room.

Bronya clapped her hands, and a shower of flower petals and porcelain rained down. "You gotta do better than that, dickhead."

Melody hummed, and everything went silent except the breathing of the girls.

"Coralie?" Markaza yelled. "Any ideas on how the hell we're gonna kick this thing's ass while he's inside my mom?"

"Working on it!"

They could see the monster raging, but couldn't hear what it was saying.

Shelia barked an order. "Melody, shift to cut me out! Keep the shield around the others!"

Her mouth continued to move, but she'd been muted.

Pamela's face went slack.

"Coralie!"

"I've got it!" As she screamed, she ran to the bookshelf and started hurling titles left and right.

"What the hell are you doing?" Markaza asked.

"Shut up! I'm looking for something!" With a triumphant yell, Coralie leapt to her feet with an old photo album in her hands. She flipped through it, hollered again, and shoved the book in Markaza's face. "Remember!"

An old photo of a mother holding an infant dominated the page. Markaza pushed the book away. "What are you playing at?"

Coralie growled and pressed the image back in her friend's face. "I said, remember! Now. Let this room fade from your awareness and think of the love you had then!"

THE MYSTIC

As Markaza focused, the noise in the room intensified.

"All of you, stop fighting! Close your eyes and remember a time you felt loved!" Coralie shouted.

It was like watching through a cloudy piece of glass. Everyone around Markaza wavered, and their lights grew brighter.

A shrill scream pierced the air, and Pamela dropped to the floor with her arms covering her head. She fell to the side and writhed, flailing her legs.

Markaza ignored her mother's shrieking as much as possible, focusing on the love remembered from childhood. Every scream was like a knife to the heart.

Black smoke that smelled like vomit rose into the air and swirled a few feet away from the girls. Spinning like a tornado, the apparition kicked up a violent wind that battered them.

Coralie's voice rose above the roaring gale. "Hold! Don't let go!"

Markaza felt her lungs scream for air as they restricted painfully in her chest. She slapped her hand over her mouth and nose, careful to keep the memories of her six-year-old self and her mother playing dress-up the focal point of all thought.

Right when Markaza felt she was going to pass out from lack of oxygen, the wind screeched to a stop, and she gasped.

Shelia was on the floor, not moving.

Melody was leaning on Bronya, who looked like she was going to puke.

Lily was standing perfectly still, her hand on her chest.

After taking stock and deciding whom to check on first, Markaza sprinted to Shelia's side and put two fingers on her neck. "Please be okay." A sigh escaped when her heartbeat was found under Markaza's fingers. "Thank God."

She turned her attention to her mother, lying in the fetal position, whimpering.

Coralie was the only other person up and moving about.

"Please, get them back to the suite. I gotta tend to this."

She nodded and started to move, but her elbow was caught by Markaza.

"And, if you don't mind, check with Nancy about the maid. Find out what happened, and if she thinks we can cover this up somehow."

"Will do." Coralie gathered the other girls, Bronya carrying Shelia, and led them out the door.

Markaza turned and knelt on the floor by her mother, brushing her hair back off her face. "Mom?"

Pamela's eyelids fluttered, and she sighed before she started to snore.

Tears filled Markaza's eyes as the memory of a loving mother faded. Standing up, Markaza surveyed the damage and let out a low whistle. Everything was broken. She spun around to find Nancy. It didn't take long.

She was standing right outside the suite door and lifted an eyebrow when Markaza materialized.

"It's bad. I'm not sure what the maid saw or heard; she looked more terrified of us than she did of my mother. Please find out, and please have someone come clean up this mess. Pamela is asleep on the floor."

Next thing she knew, she was in Nancy's arms, being hugged fiercely.

Tears Markaza had tried so hard to hold back burst forth, and she let herself melt into the warm embrace of the only mother who'd ever tried to understand or offer comfort over the previous eleven years.

"Shh, baby, it's okay. You know I love you, right?"

Markaza nodded.

They stayed there, wrapped up in each other, until her sobbing came to a halt.

Nancy pushed the girl to arm's length and smiled. "There now. I'll take care of all this. Go get some rest. You look terrible."

A laugh escaped Markaza's mouth, and she clamped a hand over her maw.

"It's okay to laugh."

She shook her head and put her hand down. "You do so much already. I hate leaving all this to you."

Her chin was lifted until her eyes locked on a pair of brown ones not far away. "I love you. You're worth every second of everything. This shouldn't have been left on you in the first place. Your mother needs a doctor; she's not well, baby."

"I love you, too. My hope is, once all this is over, she'll snap out of it and come back to being the overbearing socialite she was before. I think the visions will stop after whatever's gonna happen, happens." She shrugged. "If not, I promise to take her to a doctor right away. I just need to deal with this first. I love her, but I don't know how—or even if—I can do anything right now."

"I know. And I'll help in any way I can. I'm not here for her; I'm here for you. You're the only child I've ever really had. I'd do anything you asked."

Markaza's eyes filled with tears again. "Look at me! I'm blubbering like an idiot. I hate asking you to do anything."

Nancy nodded. "That's why I'll do anything you ask. I know you'd never take advantage."

"Thanks."

"You're welcome. Now, scoot! I need to make some phone calls."

Markaza did as she was ordered and trudged back to her suite. When she walked in, the girls were on her with questions.

"What the hell was that?"

"Is your mom okay?"

"Was that the creature thing?"

"How did that even work?"

"What are we gonna do now?"

She held up a hand. "Yes, that was the monster. Yes, my mother's fine. I don't know how that worked. Right now, we're gonna get some rest. That took a lot out of me, and by the looks of you guys, you didn't fare much better. So, I'm going to bed, and I'll see you all in a little while."

Without giving them a chance to argue, she stalked into her room, shut the door, and collapsed on the bed where she cried herself to sleep.

Chapter Eleven

Coralie's Twenty-First

Markaza woke up early and went down to talk to Nancy about the maid and Pamela. Once certain all had been taken care of—the maid hadn't remembered a thing—Markaza went back to the suite and shared the good news with the others as the delivery guys brought in the new furniture. "Thank God she was brainwashed or something. Can you imagine her running and telling people my mother was possessed, or that you blew up a door with your hand?" she whispered.

Bronya laughed. "I can *only* imagine. That would have a major impact on business, eh?"

"Yeah, it would. We'll talk about that other *thing* later. *So*, on to another subject."

Everyone got quiet.

"I heard a very important birthday is coming up in about a week."

"No." Coralie held up her hands and backed away from the kitchen island. "No, no, no, no. Nope. No way."

Lily squealed and clapped her hands. "It's your birthday?"

Markaza answered, "Yup." She leaned closer to Lily. "Even better? It's her *twenty-first*."

That comment elicited yelps from everyone.

Melody pulled out a piece of paper and a pen. "Time to plan!"

Everyone but Coralie and Markaza gathered around, throwing out suggestions of décor, food, drinks, and the invite list.

In the living room, Coralie sat on the couch with her head in her hands, staring at the floor.

Markaza asked, "What's going on with you? Why don't you want a party?"

"I'm not really a party type of person."

"Come on. These girls need something to do, and they're excited to be doing something for you. Everyone likes birthdays."

"You don't," Coralie said.

"I have a *really* good reason, don't you think?"

"So do I."

"Then spill. What's up?" Markaza perched on the arm of the couch.

"If I talk, will you get off there? This thing's brand new."

Confused, but unwilling to argue, she moved to the chair sitting directly across the room. "Better?"

Coralie nodded. "Sorry, I just didn't have a lot of nice things growing up, you know?"

Markaza mentally slapped herself. "Yeah. I get it. Okay, so tell me about the birthday thing."

"It's a lot like the couch. I didn't really have birthdays after my parents left. Sure, I had a friend now and then give me some piece of crap they'd found somewhere; but it's not the same as having a full-on party."

"Then why not have one to make up for all the others you never got?" Markaza asked. "Let the girls go bananas. Get piles of presents! After all, come December, we may all be dead and gone."

Coralie gasped and snapped her head up.

"I'm just telling it like it is, doll. There's no reason to live in yesterday, or to be afraid of what might happen tomorrow, when you've got twenty-four hours in today to live life to the fullest." Markaza shrugged and lit a cigarette.

"And that's the sage advice from the one who does it right all the time?"

"Hell no. That's just my words of wisdom for today. I fuck up all the time. I hold grudges when I shouldn't, and I've been known to lose my temper quickly. At least I'm okay with it."

"What about your mom?"

Markaza's face got warm. "She's not herself. Yeah, I have a grudge there. I have for a long time. If she would've been a mother and not judged me so much—"

"Like you're being a daughter and not judging her?"

That stung. "Touché." She crossed her arms and leaned back in the chair. "So, what do you suggest I do for my mom?"

Coralie studied the carpet. "I don't know. Something." She sighed and fell backward, locking eyes with her friend. "I just think she's gotten a raw deal, too. After all the shit your dad did to her, she had to hide a daughter she probably wanted to show off so you wouldn't get hurt."

"Hurt?"

"Yeah. You think if people found out what you could do, that you wouldn't end up a lab experiment somewhere? Come on. Give your mom some kinda credit."

For the first time in a long time, a spot on Markaza's heart softened for her mother. She was as much a victim of circumstance as her daughter, and had only recently been afflicted by the painful, sometimes terrifying, visions. "There's probably a lot of truth in what you're saying, but do you afford your own parents the same luxury for abandoning you? It's fine to lecture me when you don't have skeletons in your closet, but do you follow your own advice?"

In a voice thick with tears, Coralie answered, "I do. I try to think of reasons they would've had to leave me behind. Even though I come up short every time, I know there has to be something. No mother could—" She choked and buried her face in her hands.

Markaza got up and moved to the seat beside her friend, wrapping her in a warm embrace. "I hear you. Okay, I'll work on forgiving Pamela—my *mom*—if you'll let us throw you a big party."

Coralie sniffed and chuckled. "An eye for an eye, huh?"

"Something like that."

"Fine." She smiled. "You know what they say?"

Markaza nodded. "I don't mind being blind." Then, she winked. "Let's get this party started!"

Giggling, they bounced to join the others in the kitchen.

No one asked if everything was okay, the two were just enveloped in the group discussion as though they'd never been gone.

Melody squealed. "You're so gonna love this! We got you…"

***

Hours later, as they all lounged around the living room, Markaza let out a sigh.

All heads turned her way, and the atmosphere sobered.

Lily asked, "We can't put off the discussion any longer, can we?"

Markaza shook her head. "I'm afraid we can't. While the maid and the mess were taken care of by Nancy—and thank God we have her to cover our asses—we need to talk about what happened and try to figure out how what we did worked." She turned sideways on the couch. "Coralie? Any insight?"

"No. I just saw what needed to be done and did it. There wasn't a flashing sign giving me an explanation or anything." Coralie chuffed. "No matter how much I wish there had been."

"Well then, does anyone else have an idea?"

Shelia answered, "I think I might." She shifted in her chair. "This is gonna sound so stupid."

"Nah. Hell, at least you've got something. I've been churning it around all day and can't come up with an explanation." Markaza grinned.

"Well, it was when we were all trying to think of a time we felt loved. I was really struggling because I was so young when my parents died, and Aunt Ivy and Uncle Melvin never seemed to want me around. You were all deep in thought, and the monster seemed to lock onto me when my hesitation to come up with anything surfaced." Shelia shuddered and tucked her hands in her lap. "It felt like I was being drained or something." Her voice dropped. "I'm not sure if that thing was trying to syphon off my soul or what, but that's what it felt like."

Markaza's brain shot into hyper drive, and she pressed for more information. "What emotion was prevalent?"

"Hate. Every time I thought about my aunt and uncle, my head filled up with what they never gave me, what I missed out on… Even Mary Alice, that lady I went to live with for a day, seemed to want me more than they ever did. I couldn't seem to let go of the hurt. My doctor says I need to work through it and realize it wasn't my fault, but I just wanted to be loved—and not the way Melvin said he loved me." Shelia's eyes were bright, and she was gripping her pants leg in two fists.

Alarm bells rang in Markaza's head. "Shelia, take a deep breath, okay?"

In and out, Shelia's chest heaving with her gasps, she gulped the calming air. After a moment, her knuckles turned pink again.

"I didn't mean to bring all that pain up. I'm sorry."

"It's okay," she whispered.

"Can you go on?"

She nodded, closed her eyes, and swallowed.

"How did you beat it?"

"I remembered Janet and Kay. Those two were the only ones who never turned their backs on me. Even though I only knew Janet for a day, she was so kind. And Kay, well, she was the only friend I had. Not once did she let Ivy run her off. When I needed a hug, Kay was the friend I asked. Right before I passed out, I was recalling a time we'd been playing with our dolls—we were about eight—and she grabbed my hand and pulled me outside to the swings. She gave me a big smile and told me I was her best friend forever. That feeling took over, and the thing let me go." Shelia had tears running down her face, and she swiped at them with the back of her hand. "I don't remember anything after that until I woke up here."

All the women had wet eyes, and the sound of noses being blown filled the room.

Lily moved to Shelia's side, sat on the arm of the chair, and wrapped an arm around her.

No one spoke for a moment, and Markaza used the quiet to sort the facts into neat rows. Shelia was focused on pain. Lily, Bronya, Coralie, and Melody probably weren't in a heightened emotional state when they first entered, but Markaza was because her mother was involved. It was personal. But why was the creature targeting Markaza in the first place? She jumped to her feet. "Pain! It feeds on pain!"

Coralie pulled her bottom lip between her teeth.

Melody asked, "Are you absolutely sure?"

"Isn't that kinda what it has to be? I had pain from seeing my mother in the state she was in, Shelia had pain remembering what happened to her, and… Wait, did any of you have pain?"

It was Bronya who answered, "Not pain, Markaza. While the things we experienced left a residual hurt, it's negligible. What those things left a lot of was hate. I feel it every day. From the discussions I've had with these women, I've gathered we all have a ton of it sitting on our shoulders like lead weights."

Markaza dropped back to the couch and slumped. "How could I have missed that?" She thought back to the conversation she'd had with Coralie the night before about judgment and grudges being held against their parents. "I think you may be right."

Bronya sat ramrod straight. "At least now we know how to beat the fucking thing."

"Oh, so we're just supposed to let go of all the shit people have done to us so we can save the world they live in! That's such bullshit!" Markaza pounded her fist on her thigh. "At this point, I'm not even sure the world is worth saving. It's such a fucked up place anyway. Why not let it all go to dust?"

Lily stood up. "You can give up and roll the hell over if you want. Fuck you. I'm doing what I can to save lives. Everyone isn't like the people who caused our pain. Yes, I have a mad hate on for those tawdry bitches and that fucker I used to date for what they did to me. But I don't blame humanity as a whole. How can you even say that?" She turned away. "Just when you think you know someone…" Vibrations from her little feet ran across the floor as she stomped her way to her room. A door closing was her last word.

Markaza felt her mouth hanging open, and glanced around the room at the others. "What in the world…"

Coralie frowned. "My guess? Captain Kurt. I think she's still in love with him. Whatever voodoo that man put on her, he did it up right. She still gets all moony when he's mentioned. But I don't really wanna be responsible for murdering billions of people, either."

"Voodoo!" Markaza snapped her fingers and sat up. "Do you guys still have your necklaces?"

"Yeah, in our rooms."

"I have a feeling those are gonna play a huge part in all this. I wish I knew *how*." She slumped again and let out a breath. "I hate not being prepared and not knowing what's coming."

Melody asked, "Didn't you say you had a vision about it? What was it?"

Markaza's mouth dried up. "I saw all of us against that monster. I told you what it looks like."

"Yeah, we *saw* a glimpse of it. But what else did your dream show you?" Melody was pressing into deep water.

Markaza wasn't sure she should scare her friends that badly, but she didn't want them going into a battle with only half the knowledge at their disposal. "Someone go get Lily, please. I'm not saying it twice."

Melody took off and returned a moment later dragging a struggling Lily by the hand. She was deposited in a chair and crossed her arms over her chest.

Over the next hour, Markaza recounted every vision she'd had since the first, and the encounter with Marie in New Orleans. There were many times the others were caught looking terrified, but they always straightened their faces when Markaza looked right at them. When she was done, no one said a word.

Bronya went to the kitchen and made coffee, and the conversation didn't resume until everyone had a cup firmly in hand.

Markaza blew on hers and took a sip. "I hate to say I told you so, but…"

Shelia cleared her throat. "So the thing, presumably, feeds on hate. We're all full of hate toward the people who did us wrong. How, exactly, are we supposed to beat it if we can't get over what was done to us?"

"Maybe that's what we should be working on instead of honing our powers. WSTW has unlimited resources. Let's do something that matters over the next month to increase awareness and kindness in our fellow man. We can have a huge gala for Coralie's birthday and celebrate giving back to people while we foster the love we have for each other right here in this room," Markaza said. Her heart was drumming against her breastbone as she waited for a response.

Lily leapt to her feet. "Hell yes! We already have a ton of stuff planned for Coralie's party, so let's just make it bigger, badder, and more freaking epic!"

Coralie put a hand on Markaza's knee. "I think that's perfect. Let's do it."

Melody snagged the notebook they had their plans written in. "I'm ready to write it all down, ladies! Give me suggestions!"

Markaza smiled. "I know just what to do."

They planned until the wee hours of the next morning.

Finally, Shelia held up a hand around three o'clock. "Okay, y'all, I've had enough. This is gonna be an amazing event, but I'm downright wore out. I gotta get some sleep."

Lily was snoring, curled up with a blanket on the couch.

"She beat me to it."

They chuckled, Markaza tucked the blanket around Lily, and everyone went to bed.

When Markaza's head hit the pillow, she was instantly sucked into a dream.

"I sssssee you." Its voice slithered across her skin like a silk sheet. "This little game of yours won't work. I'm going to win, and your planet will succumb to my thirst."

She allowed her anger to fill her up, and she stood with a straight back in the absolute dark. "Like hell you'll win!" With all the bravado she could muster, she pointed a finger in front of her. "You're not coming for me. I'm coming for you. And you damned well better be worried, because I intend to kick your ass!"

Sharp pain in the side of her head had her sitting up, clutching her right ear. When she took her fingers away, they were covered in crimson.

CHAPTER TWELVE

BENEFITS

November third dawned and chaos ensued. Everyone in the suite ran around, barking orders, making phone calls, and spilling their coffee as they jostled one another.

Over the previous month, Bronya's mad art skills, Shelia's violin accompanying Melody's voice, Lily and Coralie's connections, and Markaza's staff had been priceless.

Everyone but Nancy had worked from sun up to sun down. She'd been given a month off, with pay, to take a trip to Italy, courtesy of the girls.

It was going to be an event to remember, and the whole first floor of The Clementine had been given a major overhaul.

Banners announcing the event graced the sidewalk out front and hung from the corners of the hotel. Fliers had been passed out to everyone on the street. Maxwell's was handling the catering, and there were huge plates of hors d'oeuvres sitting in the walk-ins, waiting to be carried to guests.

In the lounge, there were displays of material focused on anti-bullying, gay rights, anorexia, child abuse, drunk driving, and depression. Maxwell's had been cleared of chairs and tables, and was covered in banners announcing the gala's title: I Heart New York – Awareness is Number One.

Markaza and the other ladies had managed to make it downstairs and were gushing over how beautiful everything looked.

Coralie squealed and pointed at a glittering sign announcing her birthday.

"Okay, okay!" Markaza clapped her hands. "You know what we have to get done today. It's time to move, ladies. I'll meet you back upstairs—where I'll have a surprise waiting—at two. Let's roll!"

Everyone scattered, and Markaza headed toward the office and the event staff meeting for the day. Her employees were waiting, huddled together in groups of four. She smiled at them. "You all know today is one of the biggest in our hotel's history. I expect you all to be on point, and if you have any questions, see Johanna. She'll be handling everything going on behind the scenes. You guys ready?"

A chorus of loud yesses blew her hair back.

"Awesome. Let's show the world why this is a five-star hotel." Every employee got a high-five as they exited.

Johanna hung back.

"Did you get the thing lined up for the ladies?" Markaza asked.

"I did. The women said they'd be here at one-thirty. Do you need me to let them in?"

"Yeah. I'm gonna go check on my mom. I'll be back in a little while."

Johanna frowned. "How's she doing?"

"She's good. Better, I think. We've been spending a little time together every day. I can see it in her eyes; she's not as unfocused as she was."

"Is she coming to the event?"

"That's what I intend to find out." They hugged and Markaza headed for the elevator. On the ride up, her nerves twanged. She didn't bother knocking on her mother's door and was shocked when Pamela was found dancing around the kitchen, singing. "Mom?"

She spun and smiled. "Oh, hi, honey!"

Markaza's stomach hit her feet. "What are you doing?"

Pamela was made up like a clown, and she was wearing nothing but a bra, a pair of panties, and a silk robe that was untied. She laughed, but it was chilling—not the sound of happy, but one of madness. "I'm making breakfast for your father!" With the spatula, she gestured toward the table.

A bunch of pillows had been stuffed into one of Markaza's dad's suits, and socks with crudely painted hands stuck out of the arms. His face was an old photograph that had been glued to a wooden spoon and jammed in the neck hole.

Markaza's hand shook as she pulled out her cell phone.

"Will you be joining us?" her mother asked.

"Sure, Mom. I just need to make a quick phone call first."

Pamela snatched the phone out of Markaza's hand and threw it in a pot of boiling water. "Now, now, we can't have that." The words came out with a growl.

Panic was rising in Markaza's throat, and she put a hand to her chest. "Mom?"

"That's my name, don't wear it out!" Pamela danced back to her burning eggs, humming.

A doctor needed to be called right away, but shock kept Markaza rooted to the spot as she watched her deranged mother kiss the photo, then straddle the chair where her "husband" sat, and put her arms around the figure.

That snapped Markaza out of her trance, and she bolted for the door. Her hand clasped the doorknob, and she turned and pulled.

Pamela's hand slammed into the door, snapping it closed. "Nah, ah, ah." She waved a finger in Markaza's face. "You haven't eaten yet."

Like a child, Markaza was dragged back to the kitchen and tied in a chair across from the monstrosity that was playing her father. Under normal circumstances, she'd fight like hell, but hurting her mother wasn't something she was willing to do… yet. Markaza racked her brain. "Uh, Mom?"

"Yes, sweetheart?"

"How am I supposed to eat with my hands tied?" She tried to put as much honey in her voice as possible.

Pamela frowned and tapped a chipped fingernail on her chin. In a moment, she pointed up. "I know! I'll feed you. I haven't done that since you were a baby." She clapped her hands like an excited child. "Won't this be fun?"

Putting everything into whatever power was there, Markaza tried one more thing. "Mom, you need to untie me and send me to bed. I'm tired, and so are you."

"You're tired, sweetheart. Let me take you to bed." With a slack face, Pamela undid the ropes, grabbed her daughter, and dragged her to her room.

Markaza struggled, but her mother seemed to have gotten a lot stronger somehow. With no other means of escape viable, Markaza spun and jabbed an elbow into Pamela's stomach, then hit her on the back of the head when she doubled over.

Again, Markaza sprinted for the door. She pulled, but there was no movement.

Laughter echoed through the foyer. "Stupid girl! I've got the key!"

Breathing hard, Markaza spun around and scanned the room. She had to find a way out so she could call for help. *Call!* Her eyes landed on the phone, and she made a beeline for it. Snatching it from the cradle, she pressed the on button and put the receiver to her ear.

There was no dial tone.

She pulled the phone away from her ear and looked. There were no lights. It didn't take her long to discover that the cord to the charger had been cut. Remembering there was another handset in her mother's room, Markaza dropped the phone and ran, praying the actual phone line was still intact.

Footsteps reverberated from the hall. "I'm coming for you," her mother sang.

Markaza skidded through the door and turned to slam it, hoping the lock had been reinstalled after Bronya blew the last one up.

No luck.

Pamela slammed into the wood from the other side and beat her fists on the door. "Open the door, darling. Mommy wants to play with you."

Using every ounce of weight, Markaza pressed her body against the door and let her forehead smack the wood as tears filled her eyes. Unable to stop the anger, she let her words flow. "Dammit, Pamela! Why? Just when everything was going so well, why'd you have to go and fuck it all up again! Why! I thought we'd be okay." She sobbed. "I thought I had my mom back." Anger replaced the pain in a millisecond, and she leapt back, allowing her mother to come in. When her face was visible, with its garish color splotches, Markaza screamed, "I hate you!"

A roar ripped through the air; it was deep and rumbling, and vibrated through every atom in the room. Pamela became a blur as she hurled her body across the small space and pinned her daughter to the ground. An oily voice rang in her ears. "Yess."

When Markaza came to, she was tied to her mother's bed with coarse rope. Uninhibited tears splashed to the pillow from the girl's eyes. There was no way to undo the damage she'd done, and she wanted to sink into the mattress and disappear.

A knocking sound came to her ears, and she perked up to listen.

Bronya. "Hello, Mrs. Turner. Is Markaza here?"

"No, she's not. I haven't seen her." It was said with the sweetest tone.

Markaza screamed.

Noise like booming thunder shook the suite, and Bronya appeared at Markaza's side. "What the fuck?"

"Please, just untie me and let's go."

One ankle was freed a moment later, and the other limbs followed shortly after.

Sitting up, Markaza massaged her wrists and ankles before trying to stand. When she did, her knees wobbled.

She was steadied by Bronya's arm. "What did your mom do to you?"

"I'm fine. Let's go. I need to call a hospital. What a day for this to happen!"

They walked toward the door, and Markaza glanced at Pamela lying on the floor.

"I don't wanna send her away, but I don't think I have a choice now." Markaza turned. "By the way, what made you come looking for me?"

"I came up to ask if you'd remembered to invite Richard. You weren't in the suite, and I couldn't find you. I hunted down Johanna, and she told me you'd gone to see your mom."

"Oh. Well, thank goodness you did. What time is it?"

Bronya chuckled. "Almost noon. So, did you?"

"Did I, what?"

"Remember to invite Richard."

"Of course." Markaza's body grew warm as she thought about seeing him again. Since Lily's admonition, Markaza had put distance between herself and Richard. She was looking forward to spending some real time with him at the party—and maybe afterward. "Oh, and would you mind ordering me a new phone?"

***

Later, after the girls had been told the whole story and Pamela had been picked up by the local asylum, Markaza shooed the girls back to their work and called Nancy to relay the information to her. She said the situation was handled beautifully and asked if she needed to come home.

"No. I got it. I just wanted to give you the story first," Markaza said.

With a light tone, Nancy said, "Okay. You know I worry about you."

"I'm fine."

"As you always are."

Markaza smiled. "Thanks. Go have fun and eat amazing food. We'll be here when you get home."

"I hope your party goes well. I love you."

"I love you, too."

Precisely at one-thirty, the doorbell rang.

Markaza strolled over and threw the door open. "Welcome, ladies! Let's get this party started!"

In a flash, the living room had been turned into a full-service salon.

When the girls showed up at two, they squealed and hugged and kissed their friend, thanking her for her thoughtfulness.

Their suite became a fog of hairspray and chatter as everyone was buffed, polished, and coiffed for the gala.

Finally, it was time to get dressed. Lily had done all the shopping, and no one got to see what they were wearing until they unzipped the garment bags the staff had delivered the previous day. Melody had pouted and threatened to sneak a look, but Lily slept on the couch and played sentry.

Shelia was nominated to go first. She unzipped the bag, and a copper colored dress with sequins around a high neck spilled out the bottom, making a puddle of molten metal on the floor. Her eyes went wide as she ran her fingers over the fabric.

Lily was close by and scooped up the shoebox, holding it out for Shelia to take. When she pulled up the lid, everyone gasped. Inside was a pair of white Christian Louboutin slingbacks with copper heels and a petite orange flower, trimmed in copper thread, over the peep-toe.

Everything fit perfectly. At Shelia's questioning look, Lily laughed and shrugged.

After all the oohs and ahhs were done, Melody demanded she be allowed to go next. Her dress was cornflower blue, strapless, and complimented her new, fuller figure nicely.

Once everyone else was dressed, Lily snatched her bag from the hook and spun toward the hallway.

"Where do you think you're going?" Bronya asked.

"Nu uh. You can see mine once it's on." Lily sauntered down the hall and disappeared into the bathroom.

"Now how the hell did she know what size we all are, or what dress would look amazing on each of us?" Coralie spun around in her short, green, A-line dress.

"She's in fashion." Shelia said it so matter-of-fact, it seemed there was no room for argument.

Melody said, "She's also been to Milan and Paris for the big shows. I bet she's seen, and worn, everything imaginable."

Markaza nodded. "Yeah, she... Holy shit."

Lily appeared from the hallway in a golden gown that was cut to her navel in the front, and dragged the floor in the back. Over her arms, and flowing from the two small straps holding the dress up, was sheer, glittery fabric that sparkled every time she moved. On her feet were clear heels with golden thread encased in the material and those ever-noticeable red soles. Every inch of her refracted light as she runway walked across the room to stand in front of the other ladies.

"Wow," Melody whispered.

Most noticeable about Lily's appearance were the scars she was showing. Lines she'd previously used her power to hide were front and center—especially the one on her chest.

Pride filled Markaza up. "Lookin' fabulous, kid. You plan to drop the façade for the entire evening?"

Lily smiled and nodded vigorously. "Tonight's about acceptance. I won't play pretend when I'm trying to tell others to be exactly who they are and demand respect for it."

They cheered, and Bronya popped the champagne.

Everyone sang "Happy Birthday" to Coralie, made a toast, and then left to go downstairs.

The Clementine was nothing short of mesmerizing, and Shelia and Melody's duet floated through the speakers.

***

Hours later, after a lot of photos, handshakes, and gift unwrapping, Markaza pulled Richard into the office, shut the door, and flipped the lock.

His eyes drank her in, and she stood still and let them. Every move he made caused her skin to tingle as if he'd caressed some part of her body.

Unable to stand it any longer, she pulled his body flush with hers.

He whispered, "Did I tell you how beautiful you look?"

"Mhm."

As if he could read her mind, he moved his lips to her ear. "Do you have any idea how much I want more from this?"

"Tell me what you want," she whispered back.

He pulled back and crushed their lips together, eliciting a moan from deep within her throat. Their tongues caressed and volleyed, each pass drawing the two more deeply into the well of desire. Inch by inch, his hands moved down her bare back.

Markaza couldn't stand it another moment, and she broke the kiss. "Please."

"Here?"

"Yes."

"Now?"

"Oh, yes. Please!"

A wicked smile played on Richard's mouth for just a moment before he sobered. "I can't."

Heat was radiating through her body, and she felt like she'd explode if they didn't make love at once. "But—"

He put a finger on her lips. "You're not eighteen yet. I may not be perfect, but I'm not taking your innocence away so young. Besides, it's against the law."

Anger replaced desire and she pulled back, sulking. "Seriously?"

His smile returned, and he pulled her arms away from her chest, draping them around his shoulders. "Yes. Seriously."

"But I thought we were more than friends."

"We are. I just can't take that step—yet."

She knew it was childish, but she wanted to throw a temper-tantrum at his reticence. Not wanting to upset him, she reined her team of emotional horses in and held fast. "I understand. I'm just afraid I won't make it past my eighteenth birthday."

Pushing her to arm's length, he smiled. "I know you are. I was thinking about that, and I thought this might make it better. At the very least, it may give you something to look forward to." He stepped back and dropped to one knee.

Markaza's mind exploded into a million pieces as her stomach tightened and her heart sped up. Breathing was difficult, and the room spun around her.

A huge diamond ring glittered from the inside of a baby blue box. "Markaza Turner, I know things have been rough lately, and we might not even be here a month from now, but I'd be the happiest man alive if you'd agree to marry me."

There was only a moment of hesitation, as she debated bringing one more person into her life that could be used against her, before she threw her arms around his neck. "Yes! Oh my God, yes!" Tears of joy and fear rolled down her face as she pulled back and held out her hand.

He slipped the ring on her finger and stood, pulling her close once again. "I love you, Markaza Turner, and I want you to be the only woman in my life for as long as I breathe in and out."

"I love you, too." She put her head on his shoulder and breathed in his scent.

"We better get back to the party before we're missed."

Markaza lifted her head and kissed him. It was different from before, softer and more fulfilling, and it left her with the drowsy feeling of being in love.

Richard took her hand and guided her to the lobby, where he extended their arms in the air and made an announcement. "We're engaged!"

The roar of the crowd was deafening, and camera flashes assaulted the couple from every direction.

Chapter Thirteen

Photo Bombs

Markaza stretched like a cat and rolled over in bed. Memories of the night before hit her, and she jerked her left hand in front of her face. There, on her finger, sat the ring Richard had given her. Light from the window sparkled off the facets of the diamond, painting rainbows on the walls like a disco ball. She shifted her hand left and right, and giggled when the spots moved.

It was going to be a beautiful day, and her heart was light as a feather as she got up and went for the kitchen and her "I fought the law, and the law won" coffee cup.

Bronya was the only one up, and she was pacing the floor, slapping a newspaper, or a magazine, or something, on her leg over and over.

"Everything okay?" Markaza asked.

Pausing and looking at her askance, Bronya answered, "I'm not sure."

Since it seemed she wasn't going to *say* what was wrong, Markaza held out a hand. "Just hand it to me, please."

After hemming and hawing, Bronya finally passed over what turned out to be a rag magazine. On the cover, under big, bold letters that read "Gala Women in Hiding – New York's Best Kept Secret," was a photo of the six ladies at the gala with an inset of a picture Markaza had forgotten about. Lily was standing in the street, glowing bright yellow, while a man held her, Bronya, and Shelia at gunpoint. All three women were clearly identifiable. "Oh, shit."

"My sentiments exactly."

"Where'd you get this?"

Bronya shrugged. "I subscribe."

"You subscribe to the New Herald Inquisitor?"

"Yeah. They always have interesting stuff about celebrities in there."

Markaza held up her hands, one still clutching the publication. "Okay, okay, no judgment from me."

"What are we gonna do?"

"I'm not sure. Let me read this thing, and we'll go from there." Snagging her cup, Markaza poured it full of coffee, added sugar and milk, and carried everything to the couch. She snuggled into a corner.

Bronya sat down, wiggling her foot and chewing a fingernail.

Markaza lifted her eyes. "Go take a shower or something. You're fidgeting me to distraction."

"Yeah, yeah, that's a good idea."

Once she was alone, she read. Everything in the magazine would've seemed like false witness to anyone on the outside, but Markaza's brain was rushing like a freight train at how much truth there was to some of it. In the article about her friends and how they were aliens from another planet, there were eyewitness accounts from none other than the ex-employees in the parking garage talking about how they were brainwashed by the women before being arrested. At the last page, she put the rag on her lap and drank her coffee as she pondered. Before she knew it, the coffee was gone, and she was no closer to an answer.

Other members of the household trickled in over the next half hour, and breakfast was ordered.

Stuffing the magazine between the couch cushions, Markaza took a deep breath. "So, did everyone enjoy the party last night?"

Shelia answered, "Oh my gosh, yes! I think I may have met someone."

"Do tell."

Her face turned red, and she picked at her fingernails. "His name's Vince, and he's really cute. He told me my dress was beautiful, but that it was me who really lit up the room."

Melody clapped her hands. "What does he look like?"

"He's really tall and has brown hair and blue eyes."

"What's his last name?" Markaza asked.

"Um, I believe he said it was Lucchese."

Bronya repeated the name a few times. "Why does that sound familiar?"

Coralie answered, "Because we're in New York, and Vince Lucchese sounds like a lot of names around here."

Markaza caught the glance thrown her way by Coralie, and silently agreed it would probably be best not to tell Shelia her new man was in the mob. It was time for a subject change. "How about you, Bronya? You were looking pretty cozy with that lady from the Gay Rights Foundation."

"Yeah, she's really cool. She was telling me about all these community awareness things they do, and how they have this awesome mixer once a month for people new to the area."

"Sweet. Sounds like you're starting to branch out." Markaza turned to Lily. "And how about you? Did you have a good time last night?"

"I did. It felt good to show the real me. What surprised me was how many people were willing to listen to my story and how many had similar ones to share."

"Melody?"

"I ran into a couple of people I knew." Melody dropped her eyes, seeming to find the sequins on her sweats interesting.

Markaza's red flag ran up the pole. "Like?"

"My mom was here."

Oh shit, oh shit, oh shit... repeated through her head like a siren. "And?"

Melody answered, "She told me she missed me and wanted me to come home."

Before Markaza could press further, Coralie took the lead. "I'm sure she did. You're her daughter, after all."

"Yeah. I guess. It just felt so... I dunno... scripted, I guess." Melody never lifted her head.

Markaza knew it wouldn't take much to send the fragile girl on a downward spiral. "Did she say anything else?"

"Yeah, she said I looked good with a few extra pounds."

It got so quiet in the room, a gnat fart would've sounded like a gong.

"It's fine. I know what she meant." Melody finally said.

"Which was?" Markaza pressed.

"She was saying I'm fat without coming out and saying the words directly."

Lily lost it. "Your mother? That was the over-processed, over-collagened, underdressed woman talking to you?"

Melody nodded.

"She wouldn't know what looked good if it came up and peed on her leg. Her dress made her ass look this big." Lily held her arms wide. "Don't even get me started on her husband. His polyester suit probably came from a second-hand store. Yeah, they may have money, but they certainly aren't classy. Why the *fuck* would she *ever* feel like she has the right to tell you what looks good? You looked like a million dollars last night. Every man turned his head when you walked by. Hell, I even saw that actor you're all gaga over—Pine something—in the crowd checking you out. On the other hand, if your mom was serious and actually meant that you look good—because you *do*—then you can disregard everything I just said." She moved back toward her chair. "Except the actor part; that was totally true."

Chuckling, Melody scanned the other women. "You know what? You guys are the most awesome friends anyone could ever ask for. I told my mother to leave me alone for a while so I can get myself together. That man she was with used to be her trainer. I guess they're together now or something. Figures. She was diddling him behind Daddy's back for years. I'm glad my daddy finally got away from her. It wouldn't surprise me if she were broke and came to me looking for money—even though she didn't dare ask. Daddy's a lawyer, and I bet she walked away with very little." She shrugged. "Yeah, so I'll be staying here a while longer. If that's okay?"

Markaza nodded. "If you think I'd let you go back to that hell you were living in without a serious fight, you're mistaken. We love having you here. I was kinda hoping you'd all stay for a long while."

"I plan to. I do wanna go home and see my grammy at some point though. Thought one or more of you might come with me," Bronya said.

"Hell yes!" Lily added.

Coralie smiled. "I wouldn't think of leaving, and I'd love to see Louisiana."

Shelia agreed.

"Glad that's settled." Markaza reached between the cushions and pulled out the magazine. "Now, I think it's time we talked about this." She slapped it on the coffee table, and the other girls gathered around to look.

They gasped.

"Oh, no. That's the picture you were talking about!" Shelia said.

"Yup. It seems we've been outed, ladies."

CHAPTER FOURTEEN

THE GOOD DOCTOR

"This sucks. I'm so sorry." Shelia's face was red, and her eyes were brimming.

"It's fine. I just hope people ignore it because it's on the front of a rag-mag and not the *New York Times*. We'll just have to wait and see." Markaza mentally crossed her fingers and prayed.

A tear rolled down Shelia's cheek. "It's my fault."

"Seriously, forget it. Let's go do something productive today. Get our minds off all this bullshit."

Bronya asked, "Don't you have a membership to a gym or something? Why don't we go blow off some steam?"

Markaza laughed. "So I can watch you blow up punching bags and confirm reports?"

"Oh… Um… Good point."

"There's a gym in the hotel. We could all hit the treadmills," Melody said.

"After our discussion a little while ago, I'm thinking maybe you should avoid physical fitness activities." Markaza winked and snapped her fingers. "I've got it! Get dressed for outdoors; we're gonna do some recon."

Once everyone had winter gear on, they walked the two blocks to the park entrance on fifth and posed for a few pictures with the statue of Duke Ellington.

"It's a little bit of a walk to the Great Hill, because we have to go all the way across the park, but it was only about a mile from the hotel. I'm not sure how close we'll be able to get to the actual site. Since we pulled our drive-by last time, I'm sure the hole has gotten bigger. Melody, did you bring the notebook?"

"It's in my bag."

"Awesome. Make a note of everything you see as far as buildings in the park, line of sight from hotels and things nearby, and paths we can use to come in or go out."

Melody nodded, and Lily pulled out a camera.

"Well, let's get to it, ladies." Markaza led the way toward East Drive.

As they walked, they chatted, took pictures like tourists, and bought off the many carts of food and beverage vendors parked along the sidewalks. It made the walk much more pleasant even though it took longer than the ten minutes it should've.

"Wow. This hot dog is killer." Bronya held the wiener out. "Anyone wanna bite?"

Melody looked at the thing like it might turn into a real dog and chew her leg off.

Bronya's lip curled, and she wagged her eyebrows. "You know you do. Come on, Melody. It's a big, hot wiener for youuuu."

"No way. Don't you know what's *in* that thing?"

"Hell yes! That's why it's soooo good!" She took a step toward her friend.

It wasn't long until they were running around—Melody squealing and waving her hands, and Bronya giving chase, trying to convince the girl just one bite wouldn't kill her.

116

Lily took pictures until she couldn't hold the camera steady anymore. She finally gave up, sat down, and held her sides while she laughed.

When Melody returned, she had leaves in her hair and chili down her front.

Bronya wasn't far behind, and she was grinning like a predator.

"Oh my goodness," Lily said between breaths. "Did you get her to take a bite?"

"You bet. Guess what? She *liked* it." Bronya gave Lily a high-five and helped her off the ground.

Everyone continued walking. They crossed East Drive, went around the North Woods, and were nearing West Drive.

"I never said I liked it." Melody argued, still trying to clean the brown splotches off her shirt.

Markaza lifted an eyebrow and smirked.

"Yeah, okay. I did like it, but I never said that."

Bronya whooped. "Your face gave you away. Oh, the way your eyes rolled back, and you licked your lips… I knew it!"

Shelia gasped, and everyone sobered as they took in the destruction of Great Hill and the police tape lining the circular sidewalk.

Dirt and chunks of rock were lining a pit reeking of burnt grass. A sickly sweet, hot tar scent mingled in, making the area unpleasant.

Markaza barked orders, breaking the trance the scene had induced. "Lily, take Bronya to use as a fake model and go all the way around this circular sidewalk. Take pictures facing outward every couple of feet. We need to know who can see this area. Melody and Coralie, see how many sidewalks join that one." She pointed to the same round sidewalk Lily and Bronya were walking on. "Those are our entry and exit points. Melody, come with me. We're gonna see if we can get closer to that hole. Girls, meet us on this side of Harlem Meer when you're done."

Everyone scattered.

Approaching the crime scene tape, Markaza glanced around and ducked under it, motioning for Melody to follow. They headed for the closest drop-off, and Markaza got on the ground to slither closer and poke her head over the edge.

Bubbly, black, viscous liquid churned and boiled a few feet down. In some of the larger stones on the left and right, there were finger-like indentions that made it appear something had tried to climb out of the pit.

Maybe it's not strong enough yet... She pushed back and rolled over.

Melody pointed to the right, her face white, and Markaza flipped on her side to look. From where she was lying on the ground, she could just make out the bottom part of letterforms carved into a boulder.

"What does it say?" she whispered.

In a shaky voice, Melody replied, "If you love it, it will die."

Markaza glanced at the ring on her finger and simultaneously thought about her mom. "We have to beat this thing."

"Shit! Run!" Melody grabbed Markaza and pulled.

Two police officers were advancing on the girls. "Halt! Police!"

Scrambling to stand, she slipped in something and plopped back to her butt. She put her hands in the air.

Melody released her friend and did the same.

One of the men approached with his hand on his pistol. "It's just a couple of teenagers." He let go of his gun and scowled.

His partner caught up. "Markaza?"

Recognizing the man as someone who worked often with Richard, Markaza smiled and wiggled her upright fingers as her brain raced to remember the officer's name. "Hey."

"What are you two doing in here? Didn't you see the tape?"

"Yeah. You know me, always sticking my nose in where it doesn't belong."

He chuckled. "Aw, put your hands down and get up. Does Detective Deveaux know what you're up to?"

She stood and brushed the dirt off her jeans. "No. I didn't tell him. I saw this hole a few months ago, and I've been curious about it ever since. Has it grown?"

"It sure has. It was only about three or four feet across when it first appeared."

"Is it connected to the tar pits?"

"Not that I'm aware of. Hey, who's this?" He ticked his head toward Melody. "How about an introduction?"

Markaza recalled his name, breathed a sigh of relief, and cleared her throat. "Of course. Sorry. Walt, this is Melody. Melody, meet Walt; he's one of the finest street cops on the force."

Walt stuck out his hand and Melody placed her fingers on his lightly. Slowly, her hand was drawn up to his mouth, and he kissed her knuckles. "It's lovely to meet you, Ms. Melody. Do you have a last name?"

She turned red as a cherry. "Acworth."

He dropped her hand. "You're *the* Melody Acworth? From Georgia?"

Face still blazing, she nodded.

"I love your work. Huge fan." Walt lifted his hand and rubbed at the back of his neck. "Hey, would you consider having dinner with me on Friday?"

"I… I…" Her eyes wide, she turned to Markaza.

With a smirk on her face and her hands on her hips, she laughed. "Don't leave the man hanging! Say yes!"

Breathing hard, Melody turned back to Walt, smiled, and locked eyes with him. "Yes. I'd love to."

"Wonderful! How does seven o'clock sound?"

"That sounds perfect."

After an awkward moment, Markaza grabbed Melody's hand. "Well, it's time we were going. Thanks for keeping the streets of New York free of crime and all that jazz. See you later!"

As they ducked under the yellow police tape, Walt's voice rose once again. "Wait a second! Where should I pick you up?"

Markaza yelled without looking back. "She's at the hotel. Just ask at the front desk." She pulled and moved her feet faster. "Don't look back; just keep walking."

Once the girls were ensconced in the trees of the North Woods, Markaza stopped and put her hands on her knees to catch her breath.

Melody seemed fine, and tilted her head to the side. "Why'd we run? I thought they were being awfully nice."

"You do know they could've arrested us, right? Walt's partner looked hella annoyed at what was going on, and I didn't want to take chances. Good thing you're cute, eighteen, and available. Explaining to Richard why I was near that hole would've been hard. He told me to stay away." Markaza snickered. "So, you got a hot date, huh?"

Again, Melody blushed. "You think he's hot?"

"Hell yes he's hot. That man could melt the panties off a hooker… if she happened to be wearing them."

"I thought so, too."

"Way to go. Walt's a sweetheart, too. He doesn't really date much." Inside, Markaza's goddess was dancing like a dervish. That was exactly the kind of confirmation Melody needed.

They exited the woods near the pond and sat on a bench. It wasn't long before the others showed up.

Lily was grinning ear-to-ear and patting her camera. "I got it. All of it. We'll just need to print these out."

Shelia said, "There are six paths leading to the circular one around Great Hill. Is that odd?"

"Is what odd?" asked Markaza.

"Well, six paths, six of us… It just struck me as strange."

"May just be a coincidence," Bronya said.

"Maybe. But Coralie had an idea when I confirmed the number. What if we attack this thing from six sides? Each of us would have a clear path to move backward on if we needed to retreat for some reason." Shelia demonstrated as she talked. "If we're next to one another and in front of trees, we won't have anywhere to go if we need to get away." She took a step back and bumped into an oak. "See? I'd have to take my eyes off whatever I'm looking at to find my way."

Markaza nodded. "Coralie?"

"I don't have a bead on a plan that'll work yet. It's too far off. There are too many variables between now and then. When I try to call it up, I get a headache from the four thousand possible lines to follow."

"I get it," Markaza said. "How about we go to Fort Clinton and do a little practicing." She stood up. "Everyone but Bronya."

Lily chortled.

Bronya frowned. "Why not me?"

"Because we're trying to be incognito. You obliterating the cannon isn't going to go unnoticed." Markaza winked.

They stepped on the platform at Fort Clinton a few minutes later. No one else was around.

"Lily, see if you can make us disappear," Markaza said.

Moving to the middle of the group of girls, Lily closed her eyes and held her hands out. Yellow light poured from her fingertips and wrapped around the group.

Coralie let out a noisy breath. "That's freaky. Why do I feel the need to hold my breath?"

Everyone laughed, and the light wavered.

"Hold on to it. Don't lose your focus no matter what happens," Markaza said.

In a few minutes, a family of four—parents with two sons—came up the steps and milled around.

Breaking away from the group, Markaza moved to stand next to one of the boys. She waved her hand in front of his face.

There was no reaction.

Leaning in close, she whispered, "Beware the ghosts of Fort Clinton."

He yelped and scuttled backward, tripping over his own feet.

Markaza put a hand over her mouth to stop the sound of her laughter escaping.

His mother rushed to his side. "Are you okay?"

"T… there was a ggg… ghost! I heard it!"

She exchanged a glance with his father and put a hand on the boy's forehead. "He feels fine."

"C… can we go? Please?"

With a shrug, the mother took his hand. "Come on. Let's go. Wilhelm!"

The other kid turned around.

"I said let's go!"

A flicker passed through the group, apparently making them visible for just a moment, and the boy Markaza had whispered to blanched. "Did you see that?" he screamed.

"See what, honey?" his mother asked.

"That group of ghosts! They were right over there!" He was pointing to the exact spot the girls were standing in.

Giving his dad a worried look, the boy's mom patted him on the head. "There's nothing there. Come on."

She led the family away.

Wilhelm's voice floated back. "Chicken! There wasn't nothing there."

"Was, too!"

"Was not!"

Lily dropped her hands and put them over her face. "Sorry. It was the name. I lost it for a second."

Markaza returned. "It's okay. I was testing a theory." She chewed her bottom lip. "Obviously, they can't see us, but they can hear us. I wonder…" Spinning around, she pointed at Melody. "Sing us into silence. I wanna test something else."

A beautiful aria filled the air, and blue light bubbled from Melody's feet to encapsulate the women before blending with the air and becoming invisible. Her voice faded to mute, but her mouth was still moving.

Markaza whispered, "Can anyone hear me?"

Shelia answered, "Yes."

Bronya, Lily, Coralie, and Melody nodded.

"What now?" Coralie asked.

"Now, we wait for a couple more human guinea pigs." Markaza grinned. Spread out and look around. Pretend to be tourists.

A little while later, a couple holding hands appeared on the platform and walked to the railing to look over the park. The man put his arm around the woman, and she put her head on his shoulder.

"Boo!" Markaza screamed. Her face was about a foot from the back of the couple's heads.

Shelia, who was standing on the other side of the platform, squealed and threw her hand to her chest.

"Well, that's just cool. I don't care who you are." Markaza walked up beside the couple and glanced at them, making eye contact with the woman. They smiled at one another, and Markaza came back to the group. "They can see me, but they sure can't hear me."

Still white as a sheet, Shelia smirked. "That wasn't funny."

Bronya smiled. "Yes it was."

"Now for a really cool test." Markaza pointed at the couple. "Shelia, make them lusty. Lily, time for us to disappear. Melody, be sure and drop Shelia out of the sound barrier."

Colors swirled and Shelia hummed.

As the girls watched, the man stiffened and turned toward the woman at his side. He glanced around as though he was making sure they were alone, and then pulled her face to his, snaking one arm around her back to pull their pelvises closer. Their skin flushed, and he slid his hand under her shirt as he moved his lips to her neck.

Markaza clapped. "Okay, that's enough. Time to go, ladies! This isn't something we need to be watching."

Shelia stopped humming.

After their group was back on the ground, Lily and Melody dropped their hands to their sides, and the colors disappeared.

"I wonder if we're the only ones who can see the colors," Coralie said.

"We must be. I don't think Doctor Love up there would've gone for it if he'd seen anything." Lily shrugged.

The ladies giggled.

"Good work today. Let's get home. I'm cold and tired, and we have a shit-ton of planning to do." Markaza's mind whirled with the possibilities.

They rode the high of their success all the way back to the hotel.

When they stepped out of the elevator, Lily gasped and put a hand to her mouth.

A man was standing outside the suite door, lifting a hand as if he was about to knock.

She dropped her arm and whispered, "Kurt?"

Chapter Fifteen

Love is in the Air

Lily and Kurt flew toward one another.

She was shedding tears, and he looked like he hadn't changed clothes or slept in a long time. They pulled up short of embracing, and he grabbed her hands in his, pulling her close.

"What are you doing here?" she asked.

"I can't believe I finally found you." He tucked a stray strand of hair behind her ear.

"What do you mean?"

"I've been looking for you ever since you ran away from me at the Ritz. Well, since about two days after. It took me that long to come to terms with everything I'd seen and process my thoughts." His eyes bored into hers as he spoke.

Markaza had stopped in her tracks, along with the others, and was watching the whole scene play out. Tears of joy were threatening in her own eyes, and she sniffed them back. "Okay, ladies. Nothing to see here. Let's give them some privacy."

As they passed, Lily mouthed *thank you*.

Markaza winked and ushered the ladies into the suite. Once the door was closed, she turned around and widened her eyes. "Did you see him? He looks terrible!"

Bronya put a hand over her heart. "That's the sweetest thing I've ever seen. So that's *the* Doctor Kurt, huh? He's a freaking hottie—even with the hobo beard! I wonder what took him so long? She watched that phone like an eagle for days."

"No, she watched that phone for about forty-eight hours; then, she changed the number," Shelia said.

Melody nodded. "I was with her when she called the phone company."

"Oh, I hope it works out!" Markaza squealed. "He's such an amazing guy."

"He broke her heart," said Melody.

"I don't think she gave him a real chance," Markaza replied. "She ran away."

"Let's make some coffee and go sit. I'm sure they won't want to be bombarded as soon as they walk through the door." Coralie opened cabinets, poured water, and got the brew going. When it was done, she poured cups and everyone moved to the couches and chairs.

They talked about everything but Lily as they waited for her to make an appearance.

Half an hour later, Lily and Kurt came through the door. Her face was blotchy, and her lips were swollen. He didn't look much better, and his beard was out of control.

She didn't speak, but led him straight down the hall and into her room, shutting the door behind them.

"Well, that was fast." Coralie laughed.

A moment later, Lily was back—sans Kurt. Plopping down on the couch, she buried her face in her hands and cried. Sobs racked her body.

No one made a move; they just let her get it out of her system.

Once she calmed down a bit, she lifted her head and smiled over a trembling bottom lip. "He loves me." Again, the tears poured from her eyes.

Everyone made a circle and embraced her, whispering words of congratulations in her ears.

Lily took a deep breath and released it. "I sent him to shave and shower. He smells horrible."

Markaza chuckled and sat back down. "Wanna tell us what happened, and how he found you?"

Nodding, Lily gushed. "He said he tried to call me every day for two weeks once he realized what it was I was showing him. I asked him why he recoiled in the hotel, and he said it was from shock and a little anger. I hurt him by not showing him my true self, and he felt deceived. But once he realized he loved me no matter what, he tried to track me down. Well, let's just say New York is a huge place." She laughed.

"You mean he's been here all this time!" Markaza squeaked.

Lily nodded. "Yup. And he said he's been walking up and down the streets, hoping to catch a glimpse of me. Barely eating, not sleeping a lot, and he wasn't even bothering to shower."

Markaza felt her mouth drop open. "How'd he find you?"

Reaching for the coffee table, Lily picked up the rag with the ladies' photo on the front. "He saw this. There's a write-up in here about the event we put on. Once he saw that, he came straight here and demanded to know where I was staying."

"That's so romantic!" Bronya said.

Shelia wiped a tear away. "You're one lucky cookie."

"Wait. Did you say you sent him to shower?" asked Coralie.

Lily nodded.

"Um… not trying to be difficult or anything, but what's he gonna wear when he gets out? His clothes were disgusting."

As if a higher power were answering Coralie's question, Kurt strolled out of the hallway in a fluffy pink robe that hit him just about mid-thigh, with a bunny embroidered on the lapel.

Lily pointed. "That."

Markaza took in the reactions of the women in the living room when they saw the hunky doctor in a quasi-dress. "Lily, I think maybe you should get his size and let one of the girls here run out and get some clothes."

Leaping to standing, Coralie ran for her room, grabbed her purse, and shot back toward the front door. "I got it," she yelled over her shoulder.

"But you don't have his measurements!" Lily shouted.

"Don't need 'em!"

Bronya and the other women looked shell-shocked.

"That's settled!" Markaza announced. "Let's order dinner!"

A food order was called down, and introductions were made. Bronya and Shelia shook hands with Kurt and returned to their seats.

Kurt sat next to Lily, pulled the fluffy robe down as far as possible, crossed his ankles, and fixed his gaze on Markaza. "Good to see you again." He turned to Melody. "And you. Looks like you're doing very well. I was nervous about letting you go, but it seems Markaza has kept her promise. You're the picture of health and beauty."

Melody turned bright red.

"Have you been keeping up with a doctor here?"

She nodded.

"Excellent!" Again, he looked at Markaza. "So, I've seen what Lily can do. Pretty incredible. Do any of you have abilities like that? And what was the rush to get back to New York? How'd that turn out?"

"How about we skip talking about magical powers for now." She chortled. "That's something we can hit after dinner. Long story."

"Okay. So what about the other stuff?"

"Well, that's something I can summarize. Coralie had been attacked—and nearly killed—by a bunch of bigots. But,

Bronya and Shelia here managed to get to her just in time. We left to meet them all at the hospital. As you can see, it turned out just fine. They caught two of the jerkoffs responsible, but they aren't talking. Court date is set for February of next year."

"Attacked?" Kurt's eyes were wide. "What for?"

"Because they didn't like the decision she made. It's not my story to tell. If you want to know more, you'll have to ask her." Markaza hoped that would shut down the conversation. Coralie might return at any moment, and Markaza knew it was never fun to walk into a room where everyone fell silent because they'd been discussing you.

"Gotcha." He pulled down the edge of the robe again as he shifted positions and pulled Lily closer. "So, why are you all here?"

Their doorbell rang.

"Can we fill you in after we eat?" asked Bronya.

He nodded. "Okay, but I *do* want to know."

Markaza gave him a smile and patted his hand as she walked by on her way to the door. "Once you know something, it's hard to un-know it. But we'll tell you."

Lily gave him a wan smile.

Right after the food cart rolled in, Coralie did, too. Her arms were full of bags from the clothing store across the street, and she dropped them by the door. "Here. Not sure what you're used to wearing, but it should all fit."

Kurt thanked her, rummaged around in the bags, and then excused himself to get dressed.

With a dreamy expression, Lily watched him walk away until he disappeared. She turned back to the girls and squealed. "Is this real?"

Bronya replied, "If not, we're all having the same dream. I'll tell you what, if I were straight, he'd be on the top of my 'hit that' list."

Lily blushed.

They converged on the cart.

"Sorry I ran out like that. My heart went out to him because I know I wouldn't want to meet a bunch of new people wearing a skimpy robe. I was embarrassed *for* the poor guy," Coralie said.

"Well, there was no need to hurry. I, for one, was enjoying the scenery," Markaza said, winking. "How about you guys?"

Shelia and Melody nodded, their faces the color of Wisconsin apples.

"Is it okay if he stays here?" Lily asked.

Markaza grinned. "You may have to beat the others off him with a stick, but sure. Since he's seen what you can do, there's no hiding now. We'll fill him in and see if he wants to be part of all this." She waved her fork around the group as she filled her plate from the dishes on the cart. Steak tips, potatoes, green beans, and rolls piled high, she reached for a bowl to snag some clam chowder. When she turned, she nearly upset her food when she ran smack into Kurt.

He steadied her but didn't let go of her hand, craning his neck to have a look. "What's this? Did you get engaged?"

She nodded.

"Congratulations! Who's the lucky fella?" His hands released hers.

"His name's Richard. You'll get to meet him soon, I'm sure." Markaza smiled and headed for the table, wondering if Richard and Kurt would get along.

While everyone ate, they filled Kurt in on some of their backgrounds, asking him questions about being a doctor and what his cases were like. He admitted to quitting right before leaving for New York, and said he'd considered applying at the hospital where Coralie had been treated.

"You should do that," Lily said. "I think it would be nice to stay in New York."

His plate empty, he sat back and patted his stomach. "I think so, too. That was an excellent dinner, ladies. Thank you."

Markaza wiggled her eyebrows. "Dessert is the best. Maxwell's is famous for it. Cheesecake."

"That sounds amazing."

"I'm making coffee. Want some?" Bronya asked him.

"I do. Thanks."

She jumped up, grabbing dishes to haul to the kitchen, and Shelia did the same.

Melody went to the sink and turned on the water. They had everything cleaned up and dessert ready in a flash.

Kurt lifted a forkful of the fluffy cheesecake and examined it on all sides before stuffing it in his mouth, chewing, rolling his eyes back in his head, and swallowing. "Mmm. That's excellent." After a few more bites, he put his fork down, leaned forward, and rested his forearms on the table. "Okay, ladies. Time to spill it."

Markaza dropped her own utensil, sat back in her chair, and panned her eyes around the table. "I don't think he needs a full recounting, just what we can do, and maybe a little demonstration. Which one of you wants to go first?" She curled the side of her mouth up in a smirk. "Pay attention, Kurt, I can guarantee you've never seen anything like this."

Bronya said, "Let's go in the living room and move the furniture out of the way. We can give him a real demo that way."

Kurt got to his feet and spread his arms wide. "I'm as ready as I'll ever be."

"Not sure you can ever be *ready* to see something like this, but we'll take your word for it, hot stuff." She sauntered by with a wink.

All the ladies had just settled in the living room when someone knocked on the door.

Markaza ran for it. "Don't do anything until I get back!" When she pulled the door open, her heart grew wings. "Richard!"

Her fiancé stepped in and wrapped her in a hug. "I missed you."

Pulling back, she gave him a light kiss on the lips. "I missed you, too." Then, she grabbed his hand, spun around, and dragged him to the living room. "Richard, this is Kurt; it's a long story we can tell you later. Kurt, meet my fiancé, Richard."

Kurt got to his feet, and the two men shook hands.

"We were just about to give a little demonstration. I think you might want to sit down for this," Markaza said. "Over here." She pulled Richard to the loveseat and plopped down.

He sat beside her and leaned in. "What are we gonna see?"

"Something I've been meaning to show you for a long, long time."

No questions were asked, but he lifted an eyebrow.

"Just watch!" Inside, her heart was racing as she imagined how he'd react to what he was about to see. *Oh well. It's time he knew the whole truth.* After one deep breath in and out, she motioned for Bronya to begin.

Chapter Sixteen

Men

Bronya lifted a hand and narrowed her eyes, scrunching her forehead up in concentration. Her body emitted a soft reddish light.

"What's she doing?" Kurt whispered.

Lily shushed him. "Just watch!"

Doors opened in the hallway, the thud of them striking the wall echoing through the sitting room. In a moment, pillows in every color of the rainbow were flying around the heads of the people seated.

Kurt and Richard were slack-jawed as they stared.

With a wave, Bronya caused all six pillows to explode, feathers raining down in every direction.

Richard leapt from his seat. "What the hell?"

Markaza jumped up and took his hand. "Please, calm down. I need you to have an open mind right now. You've been asking questions, and I'm giving you answers the only way I know how."

"But what... How...?"

"Please?"

A breath of frustrated air was released from his lungs, and he returned to his seat. "Fine. But you have a lot of explaining to do."

"I won't have to explain anything if you pay attention. I told you these ladies were special. Telling you what they can do would've gotten me committed. So, I'm letting them show you."

Arms crossed over his chest, he turned back around.

Where Bronya had been a moment before, Melody stood. She closed her eyes and tilted her head back, raising her arms to the sky. Blue fog dripped from her fingertips and puddled on the floor, getting bigger and bigger every moment. It didn't take long for the cloud to fill the room. As quickly as it appeared, it vanished.

Kurt leaned toward Lily and said something.

No words came out of his mouth.

She gave a silent laugh and widened her eyes at Melody.

"I wasn't sure I could do it, but I had to try," Melody said.

Markaza asked, "How can you talk and they can't?" But no sound came with her question. Wonder filled her. Melody had used her power without singing a single note, and it gave Markaza hope for the upcoming fight. She gave Melody a thumbs up sign.

When she dropped her arms, she giggled. "Okay, you can all talk now."

Kurt looked sick, and so did Richard.

Markaza leaned close and whispered, "Baby, you ain't seen nothin' yet."

He turned white.

Melody bowed and sat down.

Shelia took the stage and clasped her hands in front of her chest. Once she had a brightly lit orange light there, she pushed it away toward her audience. Ethereal globes floated toward each occupant and absorbed into their bodies.

Markaza was dumbstruck, and her mouth fell open. None of the women had displayed that level of control until then. As the bubble melted into her chest, a feeling of calm happiness took over, and she smiled. When she glanced at Richard, she saw a slack grin on his face. His eyes were glassy as he stared forward. A barking laugh escaped her, and it wasn't long until everyone but Shelia was doubled over.

Between gasps, Markaza managed to yell uncle.

Shelia dropped her hands, bowed, and went back to her seat.

While the light feeling diminished slightly, it didn't go away, and Markaza was grateful. It seemed the men were taking the situation much better than they had been before Shelia's display.

Lily patted Kurt on the knee and stood, gliding to the spot in the middle of the room and smiling. "Mine's a bit more tame." With exaggerated movements, she waved her hands in circles on either side of her body until they were spinning tornados of yellow light. She lifted her arms straight up, and then pushed her palms toward the ground, where sparks flew in a giant arc then rained down.

Their living room was transformed into an enchanted vale filled with old oak trees, green vines, tiny mushrooms, and a cloudless sky.

"Okay, this is damned cool," Coralie said. "I didn't know you could do all this. Holy shit! Is that a fairy?"

Tiny creatures darted to and fro amongst the limbs, stopping to smile or pitch fairy dust over the people seated.

Lily giggled and nodded. Her hair was the color of spun gold, and she had two giant wings sprouting from her back, raining sparkles on the carpet.

Kurt was staring at her with a look of astonishment and wonder on his face.

She snapped her fingers and the illusion disappeared. When she sat down, he regained his voice. "That was amazing!"

Her face turned red, and she glanced toward him. "That's how I hid my scars."

"Ohhhhhh… I thought it was only something you could do to yourself though."

With a grin, she pulled his lips to hers and melted into him.

Markaza felt the heat coming off them from where she was sitting, and she waved her hand at her face. "Woo! Take it down a degree or two. Getting hot in here."

Lily released Kurt and blushed.

He looked at Markaza. "I'm afraid to find out what you and Coralie are capable of."

"You can't really see Coralie's or mine. I'll just—"

Coralie stood quickly and waved her hands around. "Hold up! I think I understand. There's more to all this, and I'm getting a feeling I've been doing it all wrong. Let me try?"

Markaza nodded and gestured to the empty space. "All yours, babe!"

After a deep breath, Coralie rubbed her hands on her jeans and put her forefingers in the air near her head. "Stick with me, you guys. I've never done this before." Her eyes slid closed, and her fingertips turned neon green.

Richard whispered, "Why do you all have different color thingys going on?"

"I don't know. We never got that far. It's just something that happened," Markaza answered.

He nodded and chewed his bottom lip as he watched.

Pulses of light beat from Coralie's hands in the steady thump of a heart. As the drumming grew louder, the light burned more brightly. She swirled her fingers and thrust them at the wall. An image appeared, like a movie, showing each person in the room moving around the apartment.

"Give me a task," Coralie said.

Bronya yelled, "Mopping the kitchen floor!"

At once, the image changed to show several Bronyas. Only one was green. That one went to the pantry, got the mop, filled the bucket, and cleaned the floor. Four other copies of the girl were gray, and all got distracted in some way or another, never completing the task.

"That's awesome," Bronya said, with awe in her voice.

Markaza fist pumped. Finally, they could see what Coralie did. "Do you see it like this in your head?"

She nodded. "Most of the time now. As you know, when it first started, I could only see text boxes with green and gray lines."

"How'd you discover you could project like this?"

With a shrug, she answered, "I didn't know I could. Just figured I'd try." She snapped her fingers, but nothing happened. "Uh… How do I turn it off?"

Lily answered, "Just like you shut it down in your head. Stop thinking about it. Remember a line out of a book or something."

With a final ripple, the wall where the images had been went dark.

"Thanks," Coralie said. She sat back down.

Richard asked Markaza, "So we can't see anything you can do?"

"There might be one thing, but I don't really wanna use it on anyone here."

"Why not?"

"Because using it makes me feel wrong when it's not a serious situation. I don't trifle with nature." Her heart grew wings and hammered them on her breastbone. She didn't want to show him what she could do with her voice; he might never trust her again.

With puppy-dog eyes, he pleaded and begged until she gave in.

"Okay, who wants to play guinea pig?" she asked.

Kurt stood up. "I do. I want to see what it feels like." He moved to stand beside Markaza, looking like a kid turned loose in a candy store with five dollars.

Bronya said, "I'm so recording this."

Markaza faced him and felt the energy flow from her toes, up her torso, and down the entire length of her hair. It was like a low-voltage shock, and every hair on her body came to attention. Power coursing through her made her feel indestructible. With a grin, she gave directions. "Drop to all fours."

Kurt's face went loose and he got on his hands and knees.

"Crawl over to Lily and kiss her feet."

He raced across the room and peppered Lily's toes with smooches. She giggled.

"That's enough. Return to my side, but stay on the floor."

Moving at the same pace, he scuttled back to his previous position.

"Stand on your head."

After five failed attempts, Markaza took pity on him. "That's enough. Sit. Stay."

Looking proud, he wiggled into place and sat very still.

She let the power wane and walked back to her seat next to Richard.

He was looking at her like she was diseased.

"What?"

"Do you ever use that on me?"

"No."

"Markaza…"

"I said no."

"Would I even remember?"

Looking straight ahead, she answered, "Nope."

Kurt came back to himself, rose from the floor, and returned to Lily.

She gushed and fawned over him, telling him what an amazing job he did.

"I did something?"

Bronya passed them her cell phone so they could watch the video she'd taken.

He laughed at his antics and shook his head. "You ladies are really something. I bet there's a medical explanation for your abilities. I'm sure you don't want to be locked in a lab for the rest of your lives, but maybe you'd each give me a little sample of your blood to look at?" His hand rubbed the back of his neck. "When I'm employed again, of course."

Markaza leaned back in her seat and lit a cigarette, inhaling deeply before releasing and watching the smoke curl away from her. "What do you think, girls?"

"I'll do it," Lily answered.

"I dunno. Ever since this whole thing started, I've been scared someone would ask me that exact question, or try to kidnap me and force me to take part—locking me up like some criminal." Bronya's eyes were blazing. "Now, here we are on the cover of a goddamned magazine for the world to freaking see. What if that blood fell into the wrong hands? What if some company comes for us, hoping to use us—or use our blood or something to create others like us—for the wrong reasons?"

"We could ask what if all day. I promise I won't let it out of my sight." Kurt begged.

"How about we say: Once all this is over, we *consider* your request," Markaza answered.

Richard asked, "Once all *what* is over? Did I miss something?" He'd scooted farther away from Markaza, and she felt the stab of resentment over his reaction pierce her heart.

"I think it's time for you to leave," she said.

"Leave? Oh, hell no. I'm not going anywhere. I want some answers."

"You need to digest what you've seen. Maybe when"—she paused and glared at him—"*if* you come back afterward, I'll tell you."

He jumped up. "That's not fair!"

She rose to her full height and put her face in his. "Get. Out." Her arm, trembling, lifted to point her finger toward the door. "Now."

Deflated, he looked at his feet. "Please? I'm sorry."

"Just go."

"Fine!" he yelled.

The door slammed.

Markaza spun around. "Men."

Bronya asked, "Wow. Are you okay?"

"I'm fine. Goodnight ladies. I'm going to bed. It's been a long day." Markaza looked at Lily. "If you have a minute, could you start those photos printing? We'll need them in the morning, and you can fill Kurt in before then. Maybe he'll have some ideas."

She nodded.

Everyone said their goodnights and Markaza went to her room. Once she was behind closed doors, she let the feelings of hurt bloom. Richard's eyes had held the same contempt as those bitches from Hemop. Never in a million years did she think he'd look at her that way.

Falling on the bed, she pulled the ring off her finger and put it on the nightstand. No way was she wearing a symbol of love from a man who'd freaked out on her the first chance he got. Yeah, she was a weirdo, but she was an awesome weirdo with super cool powers.

"Who am I kidding?" she mumbled. "I bet they're having a fine time discussing that one out there."

Rolling over, she grabbed a pillow, snuggled up to it, and closed her eyes.

Commotion in the house had her rolling out of bed to see what was up a few minutes later. Bleary eyed, she made her way back to the living room.

Richard was standing in the kitchen, yelling, with Kurt blocking the path to the hallway.

His hands were raised. "Look, I'm not trying to be a prick. She said you needed to leave, so you need to leave. Go calm down, and come back when you've worked it out."

"Fuck you, dude! Move, or I'm going through you."

"I *know* how you feel. Do you think any of this has been easy to take? The first time I saw Lily's—"

Richard pushed the guy to the side and saw Markaza standing there. "I just wanna talk to you. Please?"

Pity filled her, and she nodded. "Fine. You have five minutes. Say whatever it is you intend to say and then leave."

As Richard crossed the room, he talked. "I've always known you were special. That's been a huge turn-on for me from day one. When I saw how you made Kurt act, I started to wonder if you'd ever used that on me." He reached her and lifted her hands with his. "I was afraid. I was stupid, and I'm sorry."

Kurt had followed Richard and stood a few feet behind him.

Markaza felt her fury ebb, and she tried to come to terms with the look she'd seen in his eyes when he saw what she could do—besides save his ass in cases by providing critical information.

He rubbed her hands, and then he paused, flipping her left one over and staring at the place his ring used to sit. "What the hell?"

"Look, you were hurt, I was hurt."

"How? You aren't the one who just found out the person you were planning to marry could make you yap like a puppy anytime she wanted!"

"I told you, I don't—"

His face hardened, and he dropped her hands. "Forget it. I'm out."

The door slammed a second time, the sound a bullet right through her heart.

CHAPTER SEVENTEEN

DECISIONS, DECISIONS

Markaza stared at the coffee table, overflowing with photographs of the building surrounding the battle arena, and sighed. Richard hadn't called, and he hadn't returned since their fight three days before. Clenching her jaw, she forced the pain back down so she wouldn't cry again and slammed her finished cigarette in the ashtray.

Bronya slapped her legs and stood up. "I, for one, am sick and tired of looking at this crap. We've been over it a billion times. Unless our master illusionist over there can make half the park disappear for the duration of God only knows how long, we're fucked. All of New York is gonna know what's going on."

Paling at the words, Lily's voice shook as she said, "I've been working on it."

"Don't worry about it, sweetie; she's just in a shitty mood. We all are," Markaza said.

"Yeah, it's not all up to you. Everyone has a part to play." Kurt shot a glare at Bronya and put an arm around Lily. He kissed her temple. "You're amazing."

She turned red as a sunburned tomato and looked at him.

After watching them for a few minutes, and feeling every bit like a peeping Tom, Markaza cleared her throat of the emotional bubble threatening to burst. Waving her hands at the mess, she asked, "Could you at least make this disappear?"

Lily chuckled.

"I'm kidding. Anywho, let's get outta here for a little while. I'm restless, and I know the rest of you must be going stir-crazy. Melody and Shelia both have dates this weekend, so why don't we fill our afternoon with shopping?" Markaza suggested.

At the word shopping, Lily lit up and started babbling about all the amazing stores nearby.

Pangs of jealousy for her relationship with a man who obviously adored her—his eyes hadn't left her since he'd arrived, and his hand was always touching her somewhere—shot through Markaza's chest. Carpet fibers suddenly became the most interesting thing on the planet.

"I don't think we have time to shop. Seriously, this thing is supposed to destroy the Earth in just a month and a half, and you're thinking about *clothes*?" Bronya paced.

"Look, it's not like I'm being insensitive about the time or anything, but we've been working our asses off and *need* a break before we end up ripping each other's heads off," Markaza answered.

"She's right," Shelia said. "I'm totally drained. I'm not sure I could make a child with an ice cream cone, new puppy, and all the toys they could ever want feel happy right now. I'm so worn out. Plus, I'm really looking forward to my date with Vince, and I'd like to look good for him. I gotta get my mind off all this." She gestured at the pictures.

Bronya just stared.

"Come on, please? I haven't been on a date since… Well, for a long time. Just stop being such a worrywart and be happy for me! Dammit! I deserve this!"

From a rigid stance, Bronya's shoulders dropped, and her hands relaxed. "I'm sorry. It just feels like I'm missing something, and it's driving me insane. I feel like, if I just keep at it, it'll hit me between the eyes." She laughed.

"I know what you mean; I've been trying to piece it together, too. Maybe if we get outta here and get some fresh air, it'll come to us. Honestly, it's super overwhelming to me right now," Shelia said.

Bronya nodded and shrugged. "Let's go then."

***

An hour later, they were in the limo, rocking out to "Girls, Girls, Girls" on the way to Saks. Johanna put them out at the front entrance and leaned against the car to wait.

Shelia turned back. "Aren't you coming?"

"Nah. Rules and all that. I gotta stay with the car," Johanna answered.

"Well, that sucks. Sorry. Guess I'll see you when we get back."

She waved a magazine in the air then lifted it back to her face.

Markaza grabbed Shelia's arm and dragged her through the doors.

They shopped.

They took pictures as they tried on clothes.

Then, they shopped some more.

Seventy-five thousand dollars later, they emerged from the store and headed toward the car with ten valets following, their arms loaded down with boxes and bags.

Shelia was carrying a small bag in her hands, and she handed it to Johanna as the girls climbed into the car. "I got you a little something," Shelia said.

Markaza smiled at the gesture, wondering how Shelia had emerged from her horrific experience as such a beautiful person on the inside. Her uncle deserved every minute of prison time for the atrocities he forced her to endure.

Johanna shut the door, and the ladies could hear her barking orders at the valets about loading the trunk properly. Once they heard the lid slam, they pressed their faces to the windows and watched her swing the tiny bag as she sauntered to the driver's door.

Markaza heard Shelia take a deep breath and whisper, "I hope she likes it."

Clunk!

Rustling filled the space, and Johanna screamed, "Oh my God! Shelia!"

A two-foot smile erupted on Shelia's face. "Do you like it?"

"Like it? I freaking love it! You shouldn't have!"

"Why not? You always drive us everywhere and make sure we have a great time, and you never get to come with us. I think you deserve a little thank you gift." Shelia was glowing.

"But Clive Christian No. 1 is like… I have no words, Shelia. Thank you!"

"It's from all of us."

Johanna sniffled. "Then, thank you all. So much."

"Okay, enough of all that." Markaza swiped at her own tears. "Let's go home!"

They sang along to "Smack That" on the way back to the hotel. Even the good doctor joined in the fun. As the song's end trailed through the car, Bronya bolted forward in her seat and smacked her palm to her forehead. "Oh my God!"

Instantly, the radio was turned down, and everyone looked at her.

Coralie asked, "What?"

"I can't believe I didn't put it together before now."

"Oh, for Pete's sake, what the hell is it?" Coralie yelled.

"Love!"

"Love? Are you kidding me?"

Bronya gestured as she explained, and her words ran together. "It's all about the love. Remember the fight in the hotel room, when we had to ditch the thoughts of hate hanging on our shoulders like water buckets filled to the brim?"

Everyone nodded.

"Well, it's not about our powers; it's all about letting go and learning to forgive the people who've done really shitty things to us. More than that, actually. We already had an idea that we had to let go of the pain, but we have to embrace love. If we can do that, we can beat this thing!"

Markaza's brain whirled. "It can't be that simple, can it?"

"There's some reason this thing has decided to erupt from the ground in the one place we'd all be together, right? And what's special about us? Well, we have more emotional baggage in our proverbial trunks than a clown car has paint smudges. Every kind of bullying, self-loathing, abusive, shitty thing has happened between the six of us. Think about it." Bronya was breathing hard.

Markaza tapped her teeth with a fingernail. "You might have something there. But, there's a flaw in your reasoning."

"What's that?"

"I'm the one who brought you all together."

"But you did that because you saw us in a vision, right?" Lily asked.

Nodding, Markaza answered, "Yeah."

"We need to talk about Richard," Lily said. "Like, the whole thing. It's not doing you any good keeping it all bottled up."

"No. I'm not gonna do it."

Lily frowned.

"Make that face at me all you want, but I'm waving all my insecurities around in the air just so you can have a look in my fucked up head." Anger bubbled up, and Markaza pushed it back down.

"You know, we aren't Richard. We're not gonna walk away because you're scary or something. We understand you. It just that we need to know where all this is coming from, too." Lily put her hand on Markaza's knee. "We love you. Trust us."

After a deep breath, she said, "It's not that I don't trust you. I'm sorry for what I said. All this shit with him is just starting to get to me." Tears broke loose, and she let them run down her face. "He hasn't called since we fought."

Kurt cocked an eyebrow. "He's a moron. You're beautiful, talented, and amazingly sweet, and I don't see any guy being able to take you for granted or treat you badly. Sometimes, guys balk when they lose the illusion of control. If he walks away because you're stronger than him, then he doesn't deserve you."

Markaza sniffed and grinned.

"Besides, he only saw you make me act like a puppy. If he'd been there the other night, when Shelia made me almost shit my pants with only her voice, he'd know who the one with the true power of suggestion is."

"That *was* pretty funny," Shelia said.

"Speak for yourself. I was the one who ended up on the crapper for half an hour." Kurt winked at her then turned back to Markaza. "I'm kidding. You're all powerful as hell. If I weren't so secure in myself, I'd be running away, too. You ladies are gonna have to find some men with a strong sense of self or lie to your significant others for the rest of your lives." He held up a hand. "And I don't suggest lying. When the truth comes out, it's quite a shock."

Lily was staring at him like a lovesick teenager.

He cupped her face in his hands. "I love you for exactly who and what you are. Don't ever change because you think it's what I want, and don't ever keep something from me because you're scared of how I might react. I want to be with you, every moment of every day, for the rest of my life. While I haven't spent a lot of time with you, I know in here"—he put a finger on her heart—"you're made of gold. I know you've been through some difficult things, and you've told me a lot of it, but I need you to know I'm here for you. No matter what happens.

"If you ever find yourself looking for that one spark of amazing in your life, I hope your thoughts turn to me."

Lily was bawling like a baby.

Their lips touched for a moment, and he smiled at everyone else in the car. "All but the love stuff goes for you ladies, too. I'm here, and I'll try my best to deal with everything."

Lots of nose blowing and hugs ensued, and Markaza's thoughts turned to Richard, wishing he'd say something that lovely to her.

Kurt cleared his throat. "Markaza, don't worry. I think he loves you, but he just needs a little while to process what he saw and how he's gonna deal with it over the long term."

Doubt eating her up, she nodded. "Thanks. I hope you're right."

***

When they got back to The Clementine, Markaza excused herself and went to the bathroom. She turned on the shower, cranked up the music, and collapsed under the spray, letting all the unshed tears burst forth and wash the hurt down the drain. Her arms found their way around her chest, and she hugged herself for all she was worth, trying to mend the tear in her heart by putting pressure on it from the outside. Everything flowed down the drain as she let it out.

As she sat there, staring at the path the water took on its way out, thinking how raw a deal she'd gotten every damned day of her life, anger boiled through her blood and replaced the pain. With a scream, her fist shot out and pounded the wall, the skin breaking open and dribbling crimson rivulets that swirled with the clear liquid before gurgling away.

Any pain the assault on the tile caused was overshadowed by the knife slicing through her heart.

Chapter Eighteen

Battle Plans

Two long weeks later, Richard still hadn't called or come by. After Markaza took her frustration out on the shower walls, she'd collapsed on her bed and slept for twenty-four hours. When she woke up, she resolved not to let the detective ruin another moment of her life. Someone would mention him, or Lily would look at Kurt with her lovesick eyes, and Markaza would swallow down the bitter taste of betrayal and move on.

Everything about the looming battle had been gone over many times. Their plan was in place, and the therapist had been paying the women a daily visit to help them work through their emotional demons before the girls had to face a living, breathing one. Each day ended with the girls drained, quiet, and slinking off to their rooms to think or sleep.

Their crude maps, plus a couple they'd downloaded from the Internet, gave them an excellent means to plan an attack.

Nervous about screwing up, Markaza was sitting at the table very early, looking over the pictures, drawings, and notebooks for the thousandth time. Her coffee cup was halfway to her mouth when someone knocked on the door. She looked around but didn't see any of the other girls, so she put the cup down and meandered to the peephole. A second later, she'd opened the door and had her arms around Nancy's neck, smothering her with love.

"Oh my. Well, I'm very glad to see you, too, baby." Nancy laughed and squeezed Markaza back. Being in the woman's arms was overwhelmingly relieving, and tears broke free like someone had bombed a dam. It wasn't long before Markaza had a bad case of the snubs. Every breath seemed harder to take than the one before, and she let herself be hugged by the one person in the world she knew loved her unconditionally.

"Baby, baby, you have to stop crying. Whatever is wrong?" Nancy held Markaza at arm's length and looked her over. Unable to answer, she just stood there and cried. "Let's get you inside."

Markaza allowed herself to be led into the apartment and to the couch. They sat, and she put her head in Nancy's lap, sobs having turned to hiccups.

"Shhh, baby. Calm down. What's got you so upset?"

"Richard," Markaza whisper-hiccupped.

"What did he do? I thought everything was going so well. Last time we talked, you two were engaged." Nancy grabbed Markaza's left hand and held it up. "But you don't have a ring on."

"We had a fight. I haven't heard from him in over two weeks."

"A fight?"

Markaza nodded.

"What happened?"

An hour was spent alternating between telling the story and bawling like a baby. Right around the time she finished, the other girls started trickling out of their rooms.

Coralie was the first. When she saw who was sitting on the couch, she squealed and hugged the woman, asking how her trip was and why she didn't tell them she was on her way back.

Nancy glanced around before answering, "I had a feeling I was needed here, and a certain someone would've tried to convince me not to come back."

"You needed a break. You've been running this hotel by yourself for so long." Markaza smiled.

"Okay, yes. I needed a break. Now I've had it, and I just want a damned hamburger." Nancy's eyes sparkled. "And you need a little advice."

Markaza's heart sped up.

"Stop being so down on your relationship. That young man loves you. I know he does because he called me every other day to check on you while you were out gathering your chicks. I think he just needs a moment to get his mind together, and he probably wants to be the best he can be. I imagine he must also be a little hurt. Your powers of suggestion aren't something you'd shared with him before, right?"

Markaza shook her head.

"See? He's just having a cooling off period. Now, here's what *I* suggest *you* do: Go put that ring back on your finger. Taking it off wasn't your smartest move. You don't divorce someone just because they piss you off, and it's the same when you're getting ready to be married. He deserves the benefit of the doubt. You were gone for months, and he waited on you. Don't be so quick to give up on people. Not everyone is going to hurt you or leave you." Nancy took a deep breath and blew out. "Call him. Make sure you aren't blowing things out of proportion. Maybe he's waiting for you to reach out. You'll never know if you don't try."

Coralie was nodding and had her arms crossed over her chest. "That's damned good advice right there. Pretty much the same thing Kurt told you—except the part about wearing the ring and calling Richard."

"Kurt?" Nancy perked up. "Who's Kurt?"

"Oh! Didn't I tell you?" Markaza squeaked.

Nancy shook her head.

"Lily's boyfriend!"

"Whaaaat? Somebody better be filling me in!"

About that time, Lily and Kurt made their entrance with Bronya trailing not too far behind. Both girls hugged Nancy, and she was introduced to the hunky doctor and his story.

"Well, my, my! Aren't you a sight for old eyes? It's a pleasure to meet you." She turned to Lily. "And hello to you, too. You got yourself quite a looker here. Not to mention a persistent one."

Lily turned pink. "Yeah, he's pretty amazing."

Markaza clapped her hands. "Okay, party's over. Nancy needs to get some rest, and we have stuff to plan."

Nancy was ushered out of the apartment, and Markaza returned to her seat at the table. She ticked her pencil on the notebook and drew a couple of doodles in the margins.

Coralie sat in the seat on Markaza's right with coffee and a bagel slathered with cream cheese. "She's right, you know. You need to put that ring back on and call him."

Holding up her bare left hand, Markaza stared at her ring finger.

"Go on. Just do it."

She slid off the chair, walked to her room, picked the ring up off the nightstand, and slid it back in place. As soon as it rested on her finger, something inside her swelled, causing her to seize the phone, unlock it, and press her thumb to Richard's face.

When he answered, she couldn't speak. She just sat there with the phone to her ear and relished the sound of his voice.

"Markaza, baby, is that you?"

"Yeah, it's me."

"I'm so sorry—"

"Stop. Please. It's me who's sorry. I should've told you everything from the beginning, and I never should've taken off this ring. I understand why you're so upset; I don't blame you for it one bit. I would've been pissed, too." After a deep breath, in and out, she continued. "Is there any way you can ever forgive me?"

"Of course I forgive you. I'm sorry I ran out the way I did. I didn't know how to handle everything going on. It's one thing to know you're psychic and have seen the end of the world; it's a whole other ballgame to know you can control peoples' actions. I just wish you'd told me before I had to look like a fool in front of everyone." He paused. "Can you ever forgive me?"

She smiled. "I love you. It goes without saying that I forgive you."

They chatted for another few minutes and made a date for that night. He planned to come over and have dinner with everyone while they filled him in on the plans.

Markaza bounced out of her room.

Bronya was in the hallway and lifted an eyebrow. "I'm guessing all's good with lover boy?"

She got a smile and a wink in response, and Markaza passed on by, her heart light as a feather. Prancing across the room, she grabbed Coralie in a fierce hug and told her thank you.

When they parted, she was smiling, and Markaza clapped her hands. "Everyone ready? Let's figure this out!"

All the ladies gathered around the table once Bronya returned from the shower. A cacophony of voices soon filled the room, everyone talking over each other.

Coralie gasped. "I see it!"

It got so quiet, a pin drop would've sounded like a gunshot. After an excruciatingly long time, Markaza couldn't take it anymore. "What?"

Everyone jumped.

Waving, Coralie made a shushing noise.

Markaza drummed her fingers on the counter, her mind zipping from one scenario to the next.

Green light filled the space, and a projector-like image appeared in the air.

Coralie pointed. "There. This is the path we have to take."

Shelia's eyes watered. "So if I do this gray one, I die?"

"Yeah, so we need to be one hundred percent sure not to let that happen."

"Okay."

"Once you're in position, don't go anywhere else. You *have* to stay put."

She nodded and pressed her lips together. It was obvious, by the shaking of her hands, the reality that someone could die—and that someone could be her—had become clear.

Markaza gave the girl a quick hug. "It'll be okay. Coralie won't let anything happen." In the back of Markaza's head was the vision she'd had about the girls dying horrid deaths at the hands—or claws, rather—of the creature. A shiver sent tingles through her limbs.

One deep, cleansing breath later, she was able to think again. She whipped out a marker and made circles on the map of the park at the head of each pathway leading to the creature's area. Each woman was assigned a position by the first letter of their name being scrawled inside the hoops.

Looking at Coralie, Markaza lifted an eyebrow. "Like this?"

"Yeah. And Kurt and Richard need to be here." Coralie gestured to the only part of the picnic area not surrounded by trees.

Markaza drew stick figures and labeled them.

"Perfect. Now, our biggest issue will be these buildings."

Of the four sides of the park, the creature chose the place nearest Manhattan Avenue to venture from its hellish dwelling. That meant some of the tallest structures, which included Towers on the Park, a huge apartment complex, were overlooking the exact place where the fight would happen. Coralie picked up the photos.

"This is impossible!" Melody said.

"Yeah, how am I supposed to make us, and that *thing*, invisible to like, fifty blocks?" Lily asked.

Markaza grimaced. She'd thought the same thing, and was perplexed about how to manage so many pairs of prying eyes. "I don't think we have to. From what I've seen, everything happens at night. If we can just shield the six of us, I think we'll have a shot."

"Okay, so how are we organizing the attack on this thing?" Bronya asked.

Coralie pointed at the map where the circles were drawn. "We stand there and wing it. All I can see is us attacking and winning if we stay put. If any of us moves, it's game over. So, adhere your feet to your own trails, ladies."

"Can you make this plan appear on the ground, or superimpose it on each of us so we'll know where to move and when to go there?" Markaza's heart was doing the butterfly dance. Why she hadn't thought of that earlier, she didn't know; but, if it was a possibility, that might be the game changer.

"Great question. I have no idea." Coralie laughed. "I guess I could try."

Bronya's hand shot in the air. "Me!"

Everyone got still and quiet while Coralie focused. Again, the green light filled the room. An image flickered around Bronya, splitting her off in several gray copies that all moved in different directions.

"Tell me a task," Coralie said.

"I wanna make coffee."

At once, the image of Bronya going toward the kitchen lit up. She followed, mimicking exactly what the carbon copy was doing, until the pot was gurgling. All copies of her faded away like ghosts.

Coralie collapsed on the floor, breathing hard.

"Are you okay?" Markaza asked, stepping up and putting a hand on her friend's back.

"Yeah. Wow. That was hard. Took a lot outta me."

"Just rest for a minute." If just projecting Bronya's actions around the room took that much out of Coralie, there was no way she'd be able to project for all of them. Markaza snapped her fingers. "In a minute, if you're feeling better, would you try one more thing for me?"

Coralie nodded and pushed herself to her feet. "My head's still swimming a little, but I'll give it a go."

"You sure?"

She nodded again.

"Try, instead of projecting all the ways she could go wrong, just giving her the one that'll make the task complete."

Lily was nodding. "Hey, that might work. Great idea!"

"Well, it'll be great if it works," Markaza said.

"I'll go this time." Melody was pale, but her mouth was set, and she looked determined. "I'd like to toast a bagel."

Coralie closed her eyes and tipped her head back. A green version of Melody headed for the kitchen, got out the toaster, and popped in a bagel. Real Melody followed.

"Never thought I'd be eating carbs," she said, chuckling.

Once the job was done, the ghost dissolved, and Coralie opened her eyes. "That was a lot easier."

"How do you feel?" Markaza crossed her fingers.

"Good. I don't notice a difference from a moment ago."

"Excellent!"

Shelia yelled, "Yes!"

They all laughed—the tension in the room lifting.

"Now we'll know what to do once we're there. All we have left to do is practice." For the first time in a long time, Markaza had a good feeling about the outcome of their impending battle.

CHAPTER NINETEEN

GEARING UP

Markaza smiled at Richard and pulled him closer. Dinner had gone well, and they'd retired to her bedroom not long after. As she looked in his eyes, her heart fluttered, and her stomach tightened. She worried about one of them not surviving her eighteenth birthday, and how they'd never have the chance to be intimate if they didn't get it on before then.

Her hand caressed his face. "Richard?"

"Yeah?"

"Are you one hundred percent positive we can't? I really want to."

He captured her hand in his and kissed her fingertips. "Not until you're eighteen."

"But, what if we don't live past then?"

As though considering the possibility for the first time, he drew his eyebrows together and frowned. "Do you really think that could happen? That one of us could die?"

"I really do." Her voice softened. "It's only a month away now."

His bottom lip was pulled between his teeth.

Riveted to the sight of that lip being released, the skin glistening, she slowly brought her mouth to his.

Softly, their lips touched, and she pressed herself against the entire length of his body, hoping to entice him into sin. His tongue found its way to hers, and her breath hitched in her throat. Heat consumed her from navel to nose as she wrapped her arms around him, tangling her fingers in his hair.

They flipped so he was above her.

He pulled back, and the smolder in his eyes made her breath quicken. Easing his hand under her shirt, he rubbed circles on her belly before putting his whole palm against her skin.

She shuddered and arched her back, pressing her stomach against his touch.

With a groan, he ground his hips against her thigh and lowered his mouth to her bellybutton.

Each kiss elicited a squeal, and he grew more fervent in his expeditions. As he moved higher and brought his body up to cover her own, her breathing increased. White lights blinded her from behind her eyelids, and she grew weightless, like she might float away from him at any moment. To ground herself, she put her hands on his head and wrapped her legs around his torso, pulling him closer.

When she did that, he threw his head back and moaned as his abs contracted.

Her toes curled, and fire raged through her veins. "Please."

His eyes met hers, and he held her gaze as he pulled his shirt over his head and threw it on the floor.

She realized she'd never seen him without a shirt on. Of all the times they'd been around one another when he'd showered, he'd never come out of the bathroom in anything less than a t-shirt and shorts. Rippling muscles flexed and relaxed beneath his skin, and his shoulders were wide and hard. Her hands got minds of their own and traversed the ridges and valleys of his body.

Breathing hard and eyes hooded, he leaned down so their faces were inches apart, mint overpowering her senses.

"Are you sure?" His voice was husky, the deep timbre fluctuating through to her core.

"Positive."

Their mouths crashed together, and time became a thing to be ignored.

***

When Markaza woke the next morning, she found herself pressed into him, his arms wrapped around her from behind. Close to her face, his hand lay open, and she glided her fingers over the soft skin before kissing his palm, enveloping it with her own, and pulling his arm more tightly around her.

"Good morning." His words tickled the hair on the back of her neck.

Smiling, she turned over and pulled his body to hers.

"Again?"

She nodded.

He growled. "Woman, you're gonna be the death of me."

***

Hours later, they emerged, hunting for coffee and breakfast.

Markaza felt her face turn red at the smirks on the mouths of the others, and she wondered if that was what people referred to as "the walk of shame."

Coralie winked, and Bronya handed over two mugs filled to the rim with the aromatic liquid of alertness.

Once Markaza had a cigarette and was settled on the couch, she felt more alive and at peace than she thought she could with the battle looming over her head.

Richard sat so their thighs were touching, and the contact sent a zing through her leg, into her belly, and down her arms.

She shivered.

After a little while, he excused himself to take a shower and get ready for work. The moment he stepped out of the room, she was bombarded with questions.

"Did you?"

"How was it?"

"Are you hurting?"

"How do you feel?"

"What happened?"

Everything combined and sounded garbled. She held up a hand. "Okay, okay, listen. Yes, we did—"

Lily squealed and clapped.

A smirk shut her down. "And I'm fine. It was lovely, if you must know. And I don't want to talk about it any further. Let's leave it at that. Please." Markaza hoped they got the point. She didn't feel like diminishing the value of her night with Richard by picking it apart or allowing others a look inside the perfect universe they'd created.

As though her words conveyed it all, the other girls calmed and sat in chairs and on the couch, chattering about everything but Markaza.

She let out a sigh of relief and joined them in the gossip.

Once Richard left, they communed around the table where their maps and photographs were.

"I think it's time to start collecting gear. We have our necklaces, and while I'm not sure what they'll do, exactly, we can count them in our arsenal of weapons. What else will we need?" Markaza looked at each girl in turn.

No one responded.

She smacked her hand on the table. "Seriously?"

Lily started, and Kurt put an arm around her. He cleared his throat. "I think we all need bulletproof vests, personally."

Markaza quirked an eyebrow at him.

"Well, you said that thing has claws, right? What if it comes down to an ability to puncture that wins or loses the fight?"

She snorted. "You haven't seen the size of those claws. I think they'd rip through a bulletproof vest like a snake gliding through water."

He blanched.

"Yeah. This thing is taller than The Clementine."

He turned green.

"And all we have are our powers. I don't think it has any weakness apart from love and forgiveness. With all our work with the shrink, we're getting there; but I wonder if it'll be enough. There are only six of us."

"Eight," he said.

She tilted her head.

"You have me, and you have Richard. Don't count us out because we aren't superheroes."

Just the idea of putting Richard in harm's way made her stomach queasy. "I want you guys to stay as far back as you can. There's no telling what that thing will do to make us angry. We've come to the conclusion it feeds off hate."

Bronya nodded.

"Well then, New York is like Candyland, huh?" Kurt asked.

Markaza widened her eyes in agreement. "Sadly."

"So we're in for the fight of our lives. And, add to that, we might all die. Perfect. Fuck. I'm gonna go call my grammy." Bronya spun and went to her room.

"How completely fucked up is it that none of the rest of us have anyone to call?" Shelia cried.

Coralie bit her lip, and Lily hugged Kurt.

Melody sighed. "Guess I should go call my parents, too. Not that they'll care, but I at least need to tell them I love them."

She walked toward her room, shoulders sagging, feet shuffling, and her head tilted toward the floor.

"I have to go to the bathroom." Coralie followed Melody down the hall.

Markaza was overcome by a fierce desire to hug her own mother; a knock at the door startled her out of her thoughts. She walked over, looked through the peephole, saw three people—two men and a woman—and asked who they were.

"It's Detective Kim, Ms. Turner. I found those people you had me looking for."

Every hair standing up, Markaza nearly peed her pants when she realized who she was looking at. She opened the door and welcomed everyone in.

Kim leaned against the kitchen island, scratching the three-day scruff on his chin. "Here they are." He waved his hand at the well-dressed couple that looked like they were terrified, standing a few feet away, clinging to one another.

Markaza raked her gaze over the pair before turning to face the detective. "Are you sure?"

"Yeah, I'm sure. We ran background checks, asked them a million questions, and even checked their fingerprints. If this isn't them, I'll cut off my right arm."

"Riiiight. If this isn't them, I'll cut off your right arm." She winked.

Kim laughed. "How will we settle this?"

"I think we just need to sit down and wait. It'll settle itself shortly."

"You got yourself a deal. Got any coffee around this place?"

Nervous energy propelled her through the kitchen as she gathered cups. "Does anyone else want coffee?" She looked at the couple; both shook their heads.

Lily sidled up and whispered, "What's going on?"

"Well, if they're who Kim says they are, you'll find out in a few minutes."

"Gee, vague much?"

Markaza lifted her brows.

Kim got his coffee and added copious amounts of sugar before plopping down on a stool and panning his eyes around the room. In a moment, before he'd even taken a sip of the sludge he'd created, he was back on his feet and moving toward the table where all the planning stuff was set out. "What's all this?" He waved the cup over the mountains of paperwork.

"Don't worry about it, Kim. That's not what I'm paying you ridiculous amounts of money to be concerned over."

"Looks like you're planning an attack or something." Leaning down, he squinted at the pictures. "This have anything to do with that hole in Central Park?"

Markaza growled. "I said stay out of it."

Holding his hands up, he backed away. "Okay, okay. It's in my nature to be curious." He grinned and scratched at his scraggly beard again.

"You need to shave. I didn't even recognize you."

"No time. I'm hot on the trail of a sixty thousand dollar bounty this week. These two just happened to fall in my lap at the right moment."

She sneered. While she liked Kim and had used him many times before, because he was the best in the private detective world, she wished he were a little more couth.

"How much longer we gotta wait?"

A toilet flush could be heard from somewhere down the hall.

Her breath got short, and her eyes locked on Coralie's door. "About sixty seconds."

Coralie came out, blowing her nose, her eyes rimmed in red. It was painfully obvious she'd been crying. When she got closer, she lifted her gaze from the floor and stopped dead in her tracks. "Mom? Dad?"

CHAPTER TWENTY

MOM AND DAD

Kim slapped the counter. "I was right!"

Markaza gave him what she hoped was her most scathing glare and focused on Coralie.

She was frozen, tissue pressed to her nose, legs poised mid-stride, and eyes as big and round as grapefruits.

There was a long, awkward silence during which no one spoke, but the woman of the couple was holding on to her husband's arm like she was drowning and he was a float. He'd turned a peculiar shade of red, and he was staring at Coralie. It seemed she'd grown fifteen heads and was spitting blood all over the carpet.

She snapped out of whatever spell she was under and continued her forward momentum, right toward the waiting couple. Once she was next to them, she spoke with a low growl. "What the *hell* are you doing here?"

Her mother was shaking, but she seemed to be giving the situation the respect it deserved by keeping her voice low. "I know we don't deserve anything from you, and we're not here to ask. We came with Detective Kim willingly."

"Why?"

She softened, and her eyes glistened. "Because we were so wrong to do what we did to you. I needed to see with my own two eyes that you were okay."

Laughter boomed through the room, and it wasn't long before Coralie was holding her sides, tears streaming down her face. When she could breathe, she managed to get words out. "Okay? You think I'm okay?" Visibly, her mirth died as fury rose. With her eyes blazing, she leaned toward the woman. "You have no idea what I've endured. Eating out of trash cans, running from the police so I didn't get stuck in a home, studying every night and day so I could make something of myself. I lived in squalor. I bit and clawed my way to the top so I'd never have to live like that again. Then, I reached my goal only to be slapped back down by my own idiotic choices and a band of fucktard assholes who decided *I* needed to be taught a lesson.

"I was raped, beaten to within an inch of my life, and would've been killed if it wasn't for my new friends. Okay? No, *mother*, I'm most certainly *not* okay. And nothing you can do will ever change that.

"But, I do have to stand here and say thank you. If you hadn't left me, I wouldn't be half the woman I am today. I'm stronger, smarter, and work harder than I ever would have otherwise. So, thank you for being a coward and walking out on me. Thank you for being the kind of mother that could turn her back on her own child at age thirteen. And thank you for taking my brother with you when you left. While I'm positive now I could've taken care of us both, it was less of a burden to only have to worry about myself.

"By the way, why *did* you take him and leave me?"

Her mother had been hammered into the floor. She was visually shrinking. Each word drove her further through the wood, and she ended up sobbing. Between hiccups, she managed to answer. "He was just... a baby. Just two. I didn't... There couldn't..." She whispered, "I'm so sorry."

"Where is he now?"

"He's at our house in Short Hills."

Coralie's eyes got huge. "You live in Short Hills, New Jersey?"

"Yes." Her mother squeaked.

"How?"

"Your father got a new job." She cowered against her husband. "That's why we moved."

Fists formed out of Coralie's hands. "If you could afford to live there, you could've afforded to take me with you." Each word seemed like it took a lot of effort, and she was shaking from holding her hands still.

Markaza intervened. "Why don't we take a few minutes? Coralie?" She snapped her fingers in front of her friend's face. "Hello?"

"What?"

"Let's go in the other room." As they walked away, Markaza looked back at Lily. "Would you please make them comfortable?" Then at Kim. "I'll be right back with the rest of your money."

They both nodded.

Once the two girls were in Markaza's room, Coralie turned. "What the fuck were you thinking, Markaza?"

"That you needed to see them, hear what they had to say, and let all that shit you just dumped back there out." As Markaza answered, she flipped open her checkbook and wrote. "Call it therapy."

"Don't you think it was my decision to make?"

"It still is. Before, you had no decision because you didn't know where they were. Now, you have the power to choose. See them, talk to them, or show them out. No matter what you do, at least you got to tell them what being alone did to you." She ripped the check out and waved it around as she talked. "Felt good, right?"

Coralie nodded.

"Do you realize what you just said out there?"

She sank to the corner of the bed. "Wow. I guess I never really thought about it before. When I was face-to-face with them, it flowed from somewhere inside me. I wanted to show them I couldn't be broken, that I was stronger than their influence."

"And you are. Look at you."

"They left me and took him."

"He was a baby."

"I know, but still."

"I understand." Markaza sat down.

"I don't know what to do."

"Well, I have to go pay Mr. Slimypants. He's a great detective, but he's such an asswipe."

They laughed, breaking the tension.

She stood up, and Coralie followed suit. When they made their appearance in the hallway, her mother stood up from her seat on the oversized chair and clutched her purse to her chest like a shield.

Lily had ushered the guests to the living room—everyone but Kim, who was looking at the maps and photographs again.

Markaza strode to the man and slapped the check in his hand before guiding him to the door. "Thank you, Mr. Kim. Your services are no longer needed."

He smiled and shook her hand. "It was a pleasure, Ms. Turner. Call me if we can do business again sometime."

As she closed the door, she wondered if asking him to find Coralie's parents had been a mistake. It was supposed to be done by her twenty-first birthday, but was probably better it happened after—judging by her reaction.

She was sitting across from her mother, who'd returned to her own seat, with arms crossed and a sour look. Grimaces betrayed Coralie's inner thoughts.

Markaza wondered how she'd feel if her parents had left her then suddenly turned up out of the blue without her ever knowing they were being sought out. She smiled. As pissy as Coralie looked, she had to be happy on the inside. Though the rage was most certainly there, and a lot of hurt over being the one left behind, she had her parents back, and that was worth more than a gold bar.

Needing to be sure Kim hadn't swiped anything, Markaza slipped back through the kitchen and examined the articles spread out on the table. Everything looked okay, but something had been moved. She twisted her head left and right, looking at the photos anew. When they were on the tower, she hadn't noticed you could see right down into the arena. One of the pictures was from an angle showing the cannon. *The cannon!*

She squeaked and clapped a hand over her mouth to avoid disturbing the others. While the actual weapon was old and would never fire again, it gave her an idea. Tucking it in the recesses of her mind, she went to join the others. Bronya and Melody had returned and been introduced to Coralie's parents, and everyone was chatting like the previous eight years had never happened.

Coralie was glowing. Literally. Green light was sparkling over her skin.

When she locked eyes with Markaza, there was information exchanged silently, and the glow dimmed before fading away.

***

Many hours later, after Coralie's parents left, she and Markaza had the chance to slip away for a moment.

"Well? How did it feel to get to see your mom and dad?"

"It felt… I'm not really sure. My insides are still a little screwed up, you know? While I'm happy they're okay, and my brother is, too, I'm not sure how to take it all."

"I get it. While I've never been through what you have, I know what it's like to have a mother that you wish would really love you for you."

They hugged.

"Thanks for hiring that detective. It's a lot easier to forgive when you're looking someone in the eye who's begging you to."

Markaza winked. "Right? But you needed that. And I need to go deal with my own mother. Soon. We can't have a bunch of unresolved shit floating around in our hearts a month from now."

"If you need me to go with you…"

"Thanks. I may take you up on that."

They embraced again, and Markaza went to her room—where Richard was waiting.

It was some time after midnight, while they were lying close to one another, that she turned to him. "Is there any way we can get SWAT to show up at Central Park on my birthday?"

CHAPTER TWENTY-ONE

HAPPY EIGHTEENTH BIRTHDAY

Screams…

Markaza shot out of bed and huddled in the corner, hands over her ears, shaking like fringe on a belly dancer's costume.

Richard was by her side in a moment, holding her, rubbing her back, and whispering soothingly.

It took her a long time to regain control of her faculties. Finally, she looked at him. Memories from the vision danced between them. His broken, bloody body lying on the asphalt, an eye dangling from its socket, and his skull gaping open on one side. Her arms found their way around his neck as she squeezed her eyes shut and pressed his body to hers for all she was worth. "I love you."

"Shhh… It'll be okay." He pet her hair. "I love you, too."

Sobs tore through her; she was certain it would be their last few hours together. Her premonition had been clear. She shook in his arms and cried so hard snot clogged her throat, making breathing problematic.

Through it all, he held on.

THE MYSTIC

When she was cried out, he picked her up and put her back on the bed, handing her a box of tissues. She pulled two out and smashed them to her face to stint the flow of water and mucus.

Not once did Richard reach up to wipe away the mess she'd left on his shirt. He just sat nearby, holding her hand, saying things that were supposed to make her feel better.

Phrases like: "I love you," "We're gonna beat this thing," "We'll come out the other end unscathed," and, maybe worst of all, "Don't worry." Every time he said one, she teared up again.

"Babe, we've been over your plan a gazillion times. Everything will go just like Coralie said it should. Everyone knows where they're supposed to be and what they're supposed to be doing. Have a little faith." He smiled.

"I'm trying. But the dream… I can't…"

"No way am I asking what you saw; I don't wanna know. All I'm saying is, you've had dreams before that didn't come true. This one, you've been working on preventing for a damned long time. Your girlfriends are amazing. Some of the stuff I've seen them do over the last few weeks is… Man, I don't think a whole country could take them down."

She chortled.

"There you are. That's my girl."

"Yeah, they're pretty amazing, huh?"

"Hell yes. Now let's go get some coffee in you before your head explodes."

Tears filled her eyes again as the words brought back the images.

He hugged her again and rubbed her back. Once her breathing regulated, he backed away and brushed his lips lightly across hers. "Let's get you caffeinated."

She smiled and let him lead her to the kitchen; all the other ladies were already gathered, drinking their coffee and munching on pastries and fruit.

Melody had a banana halfway to her mouth, and she paused with the fruit inches away from her open lips. "Markaza? You okay?"

"I'm good. Just had a rough hour or so."

"Dream?"

Markaza nodded, and her stomach twisted again.

"Sorry."

"It's okay. I don't wanna talk about it. Anybody got a cup of coffee up in here?"

Richard handed her the police cup she loved so much, and she inhaled with her nose over the rim before tilting the porcelain toward her mouth and taking a gulp.

Before Melody's questions, everyone had been chatting; afterward, they stared at the floor.

Bronya's head snapped up. "Wow. With all the crap going on, I almost forgot! Happy birthday, Markaza!"

"Thanks."

Melody, Shelia, Coralie, Lily, and Kurt all echoed the sentiment.

Lily held up a hand. "Wait! I have gifts!"

Everyone burst from the kitchen and ran to their rooms, babbling about forgetting to bring the stuff out before Markaza got up.

She smiled, drank her coffee, and leaned into Richard—who had his arms around her from behind.

Laughing and shoving one another, the girls reappeared with a bunch of boxes in their arms.

Those items were put on the kitchen counter in front of the birthday girl, and she handed Richard her cup before diving in, ripping at the pretty paper on the largest gift.

"That one's from me," Melody said.

Oodles of silk flowed from the box when Markaza peeled back the top. She gasped at the color; it was a perfect match with her hair. Gently, she lifted the garment and held it to her chest. Long trails of black and purple flowed in panels that appeared to caress one another as they made their way to the floor and puddled around her feet. Spaghetti straps from the top of the bodice went over the shoulder before crisscrossing down the scandalously low back and attaching to a swoop of fabric gathered there. "Holy shit." She spun. "Melody! I love it! Thank you so much."

Blushing, Melody lowered her head and accepted the hug from her friend.

Next, she went after the smallest package. It was wrapped in silver paper and had a tiny bow in the corner. She pulled off the adornment and stuck it on her head before ripping the covering off, throwing it on the floor, and going after the box inside with a vengeance. A black jewelry case opened to reveal a diamond skull and bone ear cuff shaped so it would lie flat along the edge of her ear with the cuff gripping the top. "Who… What? This is gorgeous!"

Shelia was beaming when she lifted her hand. "Mine. I'm so glad you like it."

"Like? No, honey, no. I *love* it."

She got a hug from Markaza, too.

By the time all the gifts were open, Markaza had a pile of stuff that included gift certificates, clothes, shoes, and scads of makeup. She sat there, surrounded by all the pretty things, with overwhelming love flowing out of her toward her friends. "You guys are awesome. It's like you know me or something."

Everyone laughed.

They cleaned up the mess while they discussed everything but the looming fight. When they were about halfway done, someone knocked at the door.

Markaza's heart grew wings, and she flew to answer. A moment later, she had her mother clasped tightly around the neck. "Mom! I'm so happy you're here."

Pamela stiffened a little, but relaxed after a minute of hugging. "Here's your gift. Nice bow." She handed over a little gift bag as she was ushered into the apartment.

"How've you been? Everything okay down the hall?"

She nodded.

"We haven't heard a lot from you the last couple of days."

"I've been busy. A lot of things around this place needed to be repaired. While you and Nancy have excellent management skills, some things need attention by someone who's been in the business as long as I have." Her hair was perfectly coiffed, her clothes pressed with smart creases, and her eyes were alert and shining.

Markaza marveled at the difference the psych hospital had made. In just a little over a month, they'd transformed Pamela back to the woman she'd been before her husband died.

"Ladies. Gentlemen." She ticked her head at the girls and guys before turning to her daughter. "I can't stay long. How about we have a cup of coffee and you open your gift before I leave?"

"Sounds amazing." Markaza snatched her empty cup off the table and got another one out of the cabinet. A moment later, fragrant brew was issuing forth from the Keurig. "Want vanilla?"

"I'd love that. Thank you."

She popped in a vanilla latte pod and hit the brew button a second time. Once the gurgling stopped, she snagged the cups and went back to sit down on one of the high-backed stools.

Pamela lifted her cup and blew on the contents before taking a delicate sip, pinky finger extended. When she put it back on the counter, she looked at her daughter. "What?"

Laughing, Markaza patted her mom's leg. "You don't have to be all prim and proper, you know. We're just having a cup of coffee in my apartment. Relax."

With a smirk, Pamela hunched her shoulders, uncrossed her ankles, spread her knees apart, and put her elbows on the counter, resting her head on one hand. "Would you prefer for me to sit like this?"

Peals of giggles floated over from the girls. They were gawking.

Markaza chuffed. "That's taking it a bit far."

Pamela straightened up and crossed her ankles again. "You have your… style, and I have mine. I don't nag you. Please, show me the same courtesy. I assure you, I'm perfectly relaxed."

"Okay. Deal. Just don't ever do that again."

"I promise. Glad we got that out of the way. Now, open your gift." She slid the little bag to her daughter.

Heart pounding and fingers trembling, with no clue why, Markaza snagged the package and stuck her hand through the tissue paper. She pulled out a key ring with some kind of fob hanging off the hoop. Turning it over in her hands, she squealed when she saw the shiny cobra logo. "Oh my God! Mom! A car?"

"That's not just any—"

"For real! A *Shelby Cobra*!"

"I thought you might want something to get around in. Johanna will be busy driving me to my social engagements now." Pamela took another sip of her coffee and almost had the cup out of her hand when she was tackle-hugged by her daughter.

"Thank you so freaking much!" When Markaza let go, she backed up, clenched the key between her hands, hopped up and down, and squealed. "Can I see it?"

"Of course you can. It's in your apartment's spot in the garage. Go. Have some fun."

"I love you, Mom!" She squeezed her mother again.

"I love you, too."

"You guys and gals wanna go check out my new ride?"

Richard and Kurt held up their hands.

Kurt said, "Go on. We'll be here. This is a girlfriend moment."

The six women rushed from the apartment and into the elevator, everyone talking over one another. By the time they got to the garage, Markaza's head was hurting from the noise. They burst from the lift when the doors opened and walked a few feet into the concrete monstrosity before something stopped them, and they all fell quiet.

It was breathtaking.

Melody sucked in a breath and exhaled in a whistle. "I've never seen anything like it."

Lavender to black, the car looked like it had been driven through purple paint that had swirled down the sides, blending in an ethereal way. On the back was a spoiler that resembled two snakes writhing together, rising from the black paint to consume one another.

Markaza took a step closer, and the others followed. When she looked through the front window, she smiled. "It matches."

Everyone gasped.

Bronya said, "Unlock the damned door so we can get in and you can take us for a spin."

Giggling, Markaza pressed a button, and the snicking sound of the doors unlocking filled the air.

A moment later, all six girls were piled in the car—four in the back, sitting on laps with heads bent at weird angles because of the lack of space, and Bronya and Markaza in the front.

She stuck the weird key in the ignition, and it roared to life, purring like a contented cat. Gently, she pressed her foot on the brake, pulled the shifter into reverse, and backed out of the parking spot.

Bronya patted the dash. "Let's see what she can do."

With a grin, Markaza put the car in drive and slammed her foot on the accelerator. Squeals and smoke filled the garage as the tires melted from the friction. They shot forward, and she slammed on the brakes when they came to the first turn, whipped around the turn, punched it again down the next straightaway, and squealed to a stop at the exit.

Her hands tingled as she hit the button to lower the blacked-out window. When the parking attendant saw her, he offered up a snappy salute and lifted the exit bar.

She peered in the rearview mirror and grinned. "Ladies, let's do this thing." A flick of her wrist and the Pussycat Dolls featuring Snoop Dog was blaring through the speakers.

After half an hour of raising hell, tearing through the streets of the city, using the girls' powers to avoid being seen, and not wreck, they pulled back in the garage and parked. She was breathing hard.

"Holy shit. Let me out!" Shelia squeaked.

Bronya leapt from the passenger's seat and jerked it forward.

Shelia was out and bent double a moment later, retching. When she was done, she straightened up and wiped her mouth. "Sorry. I guess with all the excitement today…"

Markaza waved a hand around as everyone else piled out. "It's okay. We understand."

"Need a mint?" Melody asked.

"Yeah, thanks," Shelia answered. She took one and crunched it while they made their way back to the apartment.

"That was some kind of fun!" Coralie high-fived Markaza. "Great driving."

"Thanks."

When they got back upstairs, Richard and Kurt asked them how it went.

"We had so much fun!" Coralie answered. "Markaza's a beast behind the wheel."

Richard grinned. "Probably helps that she can see what's coming now, huh?"

Markaza got warm inside as her pride bubbled up.

They'd been working on honing her skills at night after going to bed. He'd blindfold her and ask her where his hands were—which was only difficult some of the time. She'd managed to master knowing his moves before he made them. It had been fun. And sexy.

Everyone spent the rest of the day vegging on the couch, watching television, and chatting. No one addressed the elephant in the room that was stomping around, causing everyone to jump every time a phone rang or someone banged a cabinet shut.

They knew nightfall was coming soon; darkness meant finally coming face to face with the creature that had been haunting their dreams for months. No one wanted to call attention to it, lest the fear would take over.

Markaza glanced at her watch. Four o'clock. They'd be leaving in two hours.

CHAPTER TWENTY-TWO

CREATURE COMFORTS

"Anyone hungry?" Bronya asked.

No one answered; they just stared at or clutched one another.

"Hellooooo?"

There was only another hour before the alarm would sound, everyone would have to go to the park, and the apocalypse would happen. Markaza was glued to her chair, and her tongue wouldn't work.

"Guys, this is bullshit! Snap out of it. We're gonna go beat this demon bastard like a spoiled child. Y'all gotta eat though. You need the energy." Bronya stalked to the center of the room and stuck her fists on her hips. "Do not get me killed tonight! Get your scrawny asses up and in that kitchen!" One hand lifted, and she extended a finger. "Now!"

Lily clung to Kurt as they rose and walked to the table.

No one else moved.

Richard poked Markaza, and she jumped so high, he grabbed her to stop her from falling flat on her face.

"What was that for?" she asked.

"Come on. She's right. We all need to eat something. You guys have trained your asses off for tonight. You'll beat it."

Though she felt her eyes narrow, she hated herself for despising him right then. "Fine." Jerking out of his grip, she launched to her feet, stalked to the table, and slammed her butt in a chair. "Happy?"

He laughed. "Yeah, I am. Now, stop acting like a spoiled brat."

She stuck out her tongue.

"Way to take the high road, babe."

Remorse filled her up. "Sorry. I know I'm being a major bitch right now. I'm just scared."

"I know you are; we all are."

Coralie, Melody, and Shelia graced the others with their presence, and everyone picked at the food spread out before them.

Melody sighed. "You know what? Screw this. If I'm gonna die tonight, I'm gonna die happy." She grabbed a piece of bread and shoved it in her mouth. "Oh my. This is sooo good!"

That did the trick, and everyone relaxed a smidge, even going so far as to pile food on their plates and dig in.

Richard squeezed Markaza's knee under the table, and they locked eyes. Every iota of her soul wanted to crawl into his and hide there. He winked, and she felt her face get warm. *Please, let me make babies with this man someday.*

Their moment was broken when someone coughed, and attention was returned to eating. It wasn't long before the tension faded back and people started chatting with one another.

Markaza took a deep breath and let it out. The entire human race would be wiped from the planet in a matter of hours. Weight settled on her shoulders. Her stomach twisted, but she swallowed down the fear and offered up a prayer. That was something she'd been doing a lot of over the previous months, and she wondered if anyone was listening or cared. She shook herself. It wasn't the time to be pondering the existence of God—or any higher power, for that matter.

When the alarms on everyone's phones blared at exactly the same moment, she nearly face planted trying to get to hers to shut down the screeching.

"Holy mackerel! Whose bright idea was that?" Shelia panted.

"Probably not the best plan. I almost kicked it before the fight even got going," Coralie answered.

Melody was bright red and hiding her face. "It was mine."

They all laughed and patted her on the back, telling her it was all good and not to worry about it.

"Okay, everyone. Let's go," Markaza said.

Instantly, the group sobered, and all the air whooshed out of the room.

Kurt held the door as everyone marched out, single file.

At the elevator, Markaza's hand flew to her chest when the door to the apartment slammed. "Dear Jesus. Loud much?"

He grimaced. "Sorry. My bad." His face turned pink.

No one spoke again until they were at the entrance near the Duke Ellington statue.

"You all know where to go." Markaza chewed her lip. "Ladies, this way."

Before she could turn, Richard pulled her into his arms. "I love you. You've got this. Believe in yourself."

She fingered the voodoo bracelet on her left wrist behind his head. "I love you, too. I hope you're right. Go do your thing, and stay safe."

Gently, their lips met for a moment. They broke apart and walked their separate ways. If two hearts could be tied together with a bungee cord, she would've sworn theirs were. It was hard as hell to keep her feet moving toward Great Hill, and the demon she knew was waiting there to rip her to pieces and consume the world. Someone grabbed her hand, and she jerked it up as she spun around.

Lily grinned. "Sorry, thought maybe you could use a friend right now."

"Damn, girl. You scared the shit outta me. Don't sneak up on people like that."

She laughed. "I was actually being pretty loud. You lost in your head a little?"

"Yeah."

They clasped hands and held on for dear life as they continued their journey.

When the girls turned the last corner before the hill came into view, Markaza worried they were too late. Rancid fog was boiling from the hole, making it hard to see anything but the glowing red light dispersing through the miniscule droplets of mist, swirling like blood dissolving in water. It was beautiful and horrifying. She gagged on the taste in the air as it coated her tongue with the flavor of rotten fish and salt.

Lily's hand jerked, and her face turned blueish white.

"You okay?" Bronya asked.

With a nod, Lily released her grip and wiped her palms on her jeans, squaring her shoulders. "Time to do what we came here for."

Markaza rubbed her palms together and barked orders. "Coralie, if you please."

Green light flowed in with the red, making everything a rich, amber color. Copies of each young lady appeared and walked forward.

"Follow your doppelgangers, girls."

"Wait!" Shelia yelled. "I want a hug first."

Bronya was the first one in, and she was followed by the others.

"I love you guys. Just in case we don't make it out of this alive, I wanted you to know how I felt."

THE MYSTIC

They hugged Shelia back and repeated the sentiment.

Markaza wiped the moisture from her face and turned. "So begins the Battle of Great Hill. While no one in the city will see or remember it, we'll coin it as such in our memories. May swiftness be in your feet, cunning be in your heads, and love fill your hearts." She narrowed her eyes. "Let's go kick some demon ass."

Whoops resounded through the space, and the girls sprinted after their carbon copies as they disappeared in the fog.

Breathing through her nose to avoid getting odour de fish full on in her mouth, she worked her legs as fast as she could until she caught up to her doppelganger. She ran through the plan in her head again.

As soon as the creature showed itself, Lily was supposed to make everyone disappear as Melody muted the action to all onlookers. This was two-fold; SWAT would be kept in the bubbles so they could see and hear, while the creature would be blind to the ladies and police officers surrounding the park. Shelia would press bravery and love outward, making everyone feel indestructible while helping them hold on to hope. Coralie's focus was keeping the carbon copies of the girls up and running, while Markaza and Bronya hit the demon with everything they had. All that had to be done simultaneously with holding on to warm memories. The ladies couldn't waver.

Rainbows sparkled through the shroud of mist as each young lady called on her gift.

Markaza held her breath and crossed her fingers.

Hissing noises rolled over the ground, sending fog rolling away from the hole in waves that resembled breakers on the ocean. They lifted and crashed silently, billowing from the Great Hill all the way to the park's outer fence. A shadow, round on top with spikes the size of large dogs in a ridge across the top, rose slowly from the ground.

Screeching cut through the air as long talons were pulled over the rocks, signaling the arrival of the demon from Hell.

Police officers were yelling as they got their first sinister glimpse, and the most prevalent question was: What the hell is that thing?

It sniffed the air. Long, raspy breaths in and out.

As the noises grew louder, the fog dispersed, leaving everyone a perfect view of their adversary.

All the blood drained to Markaza's feet as she gazed upon the creature whipping its head back and forth, sniffing like a dog on the trail of a bone. There was the flaw in the plan. They hadn't counted on scent. She'd never seen it do that in her visions.

It's going to find us…

Chapter Twenty-Three

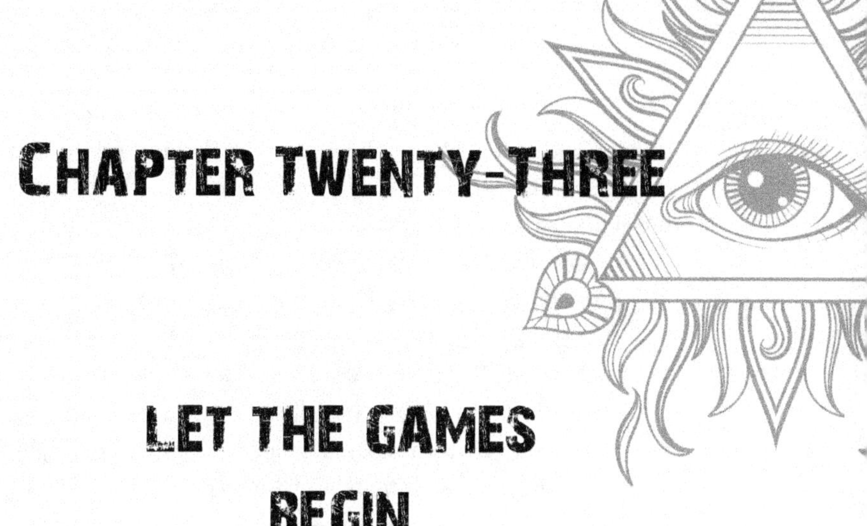

Let the Games Begin

Markaza could hear the policemen running, and she focused her attention on the beast being birthed from the soil. It continued its hunt, which told her Melody's sound barrier was working.

Out of nowhere, a blazing trail of flame shot past, colliding with the monster's hide before exploding in a dazzling spray of sparks and smoke. Two long protrusions were lifted over the creature's head, and it roared with anger.

Markaza screamed, "It's about to attack. Watch the trees!"

Talons cut through stately oaks, severing tops and sending branches crashing to the ground.

Red light appeared on the other side of the clearing as Bronya deflected the projectiles.

But the invisibility barrier wavered for a fraction of a second.

"I knew you would come." Its voice slithered over the park, sending frost that clung to the blades of grass. "You cannot stop me, girl!" Again, claws ripped through the area, sending chunks of concrete flying. "I sssaw you."

"Take that, you piece of shit!" Bronya screamed as she pounded her fist toward the ground, hitting the creature in the center of its back, making it howl. Her fist shot toward the sky, and the sound of teeth being slammed together ricocheted as the monster's head snapped back.

It chuckled. "Isss that the best you can do?"

Limbs rose from the ground, becoming deadly spikes that flew at the beast's body. As though the branches of the oaks were bothersome flies, they were swatted away.

"My turn." It opened its mouth and all the ladies watched, frozen in terror, as huge fangs descended from its upper jaw. Like a spitting cobra, venom was sprayed into the clearing nearby.

Markaza sucked in air as she watched the acidic liquid sizzle and boil on the grass, grateful none of her friends had been standing there.

Lights, small baubles in different colors, rose from the ground and assaulted the creature, pounding it in the face, popping in its eyes, and dodging well-aimed blows by its fists.

"What isss this magic?"

She fist pumped. It seemed Lily was creating a bit of a diversion.

Bronya attacked again, and more rockets were fired by SWAT.

In extreme annoyance, the demon bellowed its rage into the night air.

People weren't running out of apartments or screaming through the streets, and Markaza took that as a sign the wards were working. She yelled, "Melody, it needs to hear me. Just me!"

After a moment, she tried speaking while the others kept up their attacks. "You won't win this fight. It's better to give up now."

Shelia's voice joined in, and Markaza breathed a sigh of relief for the unexpected help even as her ire grew at Melody for not listening.

A shrill whistle pierced the air, forcing the girls to cover their ears. "No. You sshall not use that power on me."

Melody's voice followed shortly after blessed silence. "You two okay?"

"Yes!" came from the other side of the clearing.

Relief lifted weight from Markaza's chest. "I'm good. Sorry, I didn't know it could do that!"

Bronya was still punching and kicking, but her movements were slowing down. Sweat glistened on her brow.

"Bronya, stop for a minute!" Markaza yelled. "Take a breather. This isn't working. We need a new plan."

"No! Keep doing what you're doing," Coralie said. "I see us winning if we stay on this path."

"How?"

"I have no idea! I just see the thing dying in a sizzling pile of freaking goo, okay?"

One deep breath later, Markaza came up with a new plan, and she yelled it to the other women.

At once, they could no longer hear the creature.

"Can you hear me?" she said, quietly.

Its head spun toward her.

"Guess that's a yes."

Greasy lips pulled back to reveal rows of sharp white teeth with pointy tips, fangs still extended, dripping clear liquid on the ground. A forked tongue darted out, tasting the air. The thing's lips moved, but it had been rendered mute.

"You should give up. We're going to beat you. There's nothing here you want."

Again, Shelia's voice harmonized with Markaza's, and the creature lifted its snout toward the air like it had before. But the girls kept repeating their words. It wasn't long before the beast started to wilt like a wildflower deprived of rain.

"Now, Bronya!"

Thrashing ensued that shook the entire park as Bronya rained blow after devastating blow on the thing's head. It screeched and bayed as it was beaten. Finally, they were getting somewhere.

Suddenly, the red light in the hole brightened to supernova proportions. It blasted in every direction, and the demon planted its hands on the ground and shoved, pulling a bumpy, black, shiny body out of the ground. Tar dripped off in gargantuan amounts that splattered as they hit the ground, covering everything within a five-foot radius in murky goo.

Everyone stopped fighting as they paused to stare at the scene unfolding on Great Hill.

Just when it seemed the creature's body was coming to an end, more rose from the hole. Finally, a leathery foot with three talons was pulled from the quagmire and slammed down.

Markaza felt her mouth drop open as her gaze raked up the thing's body. Her neck craned to see the head, towering above the buildings surrounding the park. "Oh, fun."

"We're fucked!" Bronya yelled. "This thing is freaking *huge!*"

A shock wave rolled over the ground when the second foot made contact. All illusions flickered and went out.

"Lily!" Shelia's voice rose above the sounds of hundreds of armed men toppling.

"Do *not* move!" Coralie ordered. "Stay with your doppelganger."

Markaza watched, helplessly, as Shelia darted from her path toward Lily—leaning on a tree with her head between her knees.

A clawed hand reached down and picked Shelia up, shaking her. She screamed and threw her arms over her head as she was moved toward the venomous mouth.

Richard burst from the shadows, running toward the demon, screaming curses and yelling, "Over here!"

"Stop." Markaza put every ounce of her power into the command.

His feet slowed, then stilled.

"Turn around and go back the way you came."

He spun but was hit from behind as he took the first step.

She watched him sail across the grass and come to a stop about fifty yards out. He didn't move again. Anger rose in her like a volcanic eruption, and she turned on the creature. "That's the last straw, dickhead." Her body went ramrod straight as she stacked her spine and drew power from the Earth's energy. "You've screwed with my life long enough! I'm sick and fucking tired of beating you out of my head. It's time for   " Pain sliced through her wrist where the bracelet from Marie hung. Blood flowed down Markaza's fingers and dripped on the grass near her feet. "What the hell?" She lifted the limb to look at her damaged arm. "How did that happen?" Recalling a section about blood sacrifices from her voodoo book, she gasped, worried about what might happen next. It wasn't disappointing.

People swarmed into the park from every direction, eyes solid white and staring. They gathered near the battleground, forming a wall of bodies.

"What's this?" The demon asked.

With no answer handy, Markaza had no idea how to respond—she didn't even have a good comeback. She stood there, dumbfounded.

Shelia's limp body hung in the creature's hand, her arms and legs wagging every time it gestured, now and then a hand or foot coming in contact with a drop of poison. Odors of burning flesh wafted across the park. Markaza tracked the movements with her eyes, willing the demon to drop its prisoner.

"America the Beautiful" started quietly, and gradually gained volume as more of the people gathered joined in.

"Holy shit," she whispered.

Putrid bubbles popped on the creature's flesh, and it screamed in agony.

Shelia fell.

"Bronya!" Markaza screamed. "Catch her!"

Tiny red lights that looked like radioactive fireflies whizzed through the air in a cloud, creating a cushion that guided Shelia safely, and gently, to the ground.

"Now! Attack!"

Rockets blasted through the clearing, striking the monster in several of the wounds created by the bursting pustules. It bellowed a roar.

Bronya lifted her hands together, facing away from one another, and forced them apart.

One of the demon's legs split down the middle, spraying blood over the people on the ground. An agonizing wail permeated the park, followed by a shrill whistle that brought immediate silence.

Everyone had their hands over their ears, but Melody's voice still came through loud and clear. She was singing for her life, and Markaza's heart swelled with love and pride.

Gradually, the whistling sound diminished before stopping altogether. Again, the crowd resumed their music of love, arms around one another, swaying to and fro.

"You will find nothing but love and brotherhood here." Around Markaza's neck, the stone in the necklace got hot. She smelled burning skin, but refused to stop her assault. "There is no way to win."

A long, greasy looking arm spiraled through the darkness, taking down a whole row of apartment buildings. Bodies flew from the destruction in every direction, some ripped to pieces as the monster flailed.

Unable to watch, she lowered her eyelids and allowed her power to consume her as she continued her verbal assault.

New Yorkers kept flooding into the clearing, their voices mingling together, creating a wave of pride and love that tore the being apart every time the emotions crashed over it.

A new feeling rose in her, and she embraced it like a long lost sister. Words she knew had to be spoken by all flooded her mind, and she projected them to the crowd with a directive. "Repeat these words:

If spirits threaten me in this place,

fight water by water and fire by fire,

banish their souls into nothingness,

and remove their powers until the last trace.

Let these evil beings flee,

through time and space.

We love one another,

and will not be beat."

As the incantation left her lips, she felt tremors flow down her body and out toward the demon.

Like the collective army they were, the people of the city repeated the words, but they did it in song. Everyone lifted their arms in the air, palms toward the creature.

Markaza's eyes snapped open when she heard Shelia's voice join in. "Shelia! Don't do it! Save your strength!"

But she didn't listen. She lifted her head and sang, her body glowing the brightest orange it had been yet. Clumsily, she tried to stand, but fell when her leg split and bent at an odd angle. "I love you, Markaza, and I love the world." Her body crumbled to a heap.

Unable to move, all Markaza could do was watch as the life force left her friend and floated away on the breeze. There was no way to go to her, hold her, or cry for her as she died, and Markaza felt her heart break behind her sternum as rivers of tears burst from her eyes and she fell to her knees.

None of the other ladies seemed to have noticed, and she didn't call attention to their loss for fear it would destroy the hold they'd managed to gain on the monster. But Markaza could weep, and she did. The creature was jerking as its body disintegrated and peeled away, falling back into the stinking hole on Great Hill.

SWAT was still attacking, and gunshots rang out to mingle with the sounds of rockets.

Bronya was weakening and could only manage to pound the beast once every few minutes.

Roars suddenly filled the air as Melody's powers shut down.

"Ladies, put your hands around the stones at your necks, close your eyes, and concentrate. Let the Earth's energy refill your bodies and replenish your minds," Markaza said. "Then, sing. Love one another. Love this city. Love everyone who's ever done you wrong. Let it flow, and direct it toward that thing." She wiped the tears from her eyes so everything would clear and stood up on wobbly legs. In a flash of vision, she saw it coming before it connected and lurched left to avoid a blow aimed at her head by the demon.

Its face moved to within an inch of her own, and its breath fanned over her as it spoke. "I am immortal. I am hate."

Fury had her narrowing her eyes at the red orbs boring into her, searching for residual hate stains on her soul. She felt the probing fingers, pushing, prodding at her heart. "And when you come back, humanity will still be here."

"I am counting on that."

Her lips curled in a sneer she felt all the way to her fingertips. "What you don't seem to understand is that humanity isn't something to be preyed upon. We may be bastards to one another, have wars for supremacy, and be full of emotion all the time, but when it comes to survival, we'll always come together to stand against a piece of shit like you." She spit on the thing's snout, pulled out her switchblade, snapped it open, and stabbed the forked tongue.

THE MYSTIC

The creature's eyes widened, and it grimaced as the assault on its body by the others continued. "Puny fool. I will kill you all. When I am done—"

Another creature, blinding white light pouring off its skin, rose behind the black one, extending glowing arms that snaked around the dark demon's torso, cutting off the promise.

It spun and lashed at the newcomer, claws passing right through the ethereal light. "You shall not take me!"

Yellow brilliance radiated from Lily's position, and it was joined by light in blue, red, and green. As the colors mingled, they shot toward the white beast.

"No!" Markaza screamed. Then, she clamped a hand over her mouth. Down the thing's limbs the colors traveled, after being absorbed into its chest, seeming to make their ally more substantial with each addition.

Long, red, curly vines grew from spindly fingers and wrapped around the chunky garbage hide of the nightmare demon. It hissed and threw back its head in a scream as it struggled to break free of the magical snare.

"Markaza, we kinda need your help here," Bronya said, through gritted teeth.

Snapping out of the awe the girls had induced, Markaza clenched the burning hot necklace and added her power to the collective energy flowing into the new apparition. A smell like blooming gardenias flowed up her nose, drowning out the acrid stench. She inhaled, letting the scent fill her up from, and pressed the feeling toward the white creature.

Voices rose and blended together all around her. Blood trickled off her elbow from the spot where the bones of the bracelet had pierced her wrist. She felt alive and powerful, reveling in the energy from her friends as it intermingled with her own.

There was no break in the assault as the people of the city fought with their hearts to heal the rift opened by cruelty and loathing. Love flowed, rustling the grass with the intensity in which it sped toward the being writhing in the grip of its opponent.

As she watched, the white creature enveloped the black one and pulled it down—howling and clawing at the ground—into the tar. A huge bubble rose from the pit and burst with a hiss as steaming stickiness was sprayed into the air.

All light faded, and she could see her friends standing in their places around the circle. She smiled as her gaze passed over them until it came to rest on Shelia.

Without a thought, Markaza rushed toward the girl's still body.

Coralie screamed, "Nooooo!"

Markaza's feet stopped their forward momentum, but it was too late, she was too close.

A long tendril whipped out of the pit, seizing Markaza's ankle, knocking her off her feet and dragging her toward the rent in the earth. Her fingers scrabbled on the ground as she tried to find purchase, something to stop the backward momentum. Furrows were created in the dirt as she clawed at the grass, ripping it up in chunks. She kicked at the thing pulling her, but it had wound up her leg all the way to the knee. There was a moment of clarity where she knew it was the end, and her heart clenched in her chest as she was dragged under the quagmire.

CHAPTER TWENTY-FOUR

AFTERLIFE

Floating.

Markaza flapped her arms, trying to propel her body in some kind of direction. But everything was black, robbing her of her most precious sense. Instead of trying to see, she opened herself up to feeling, hearing, and smelling.

It felt like falling, but her clothes and hair weren't moving. Nothing was in the air; not a bird chirp, a grass scent, or the sounds of people milling about that was there a moment before. She patted her arms and legs, but she couldn't find an injury. Even the thing that had been squeezing her ankle had gone.

Am I dead?

From somewhere, a soft, whispery voice answered, "Yes. You're in the afterlife."

Remembering her friends and Richard, Markaza felt the pangs of regret for leaving them so suddenly stab her in the stomach. He wouldn't understand why she moved. No one but her had seen Shelia give her last breath to save them all. What a true jewel of humanity that girl was. Sparkles filled the air around Markaza, the only light in the gloom. A lit outline grew in front of her, slowly creating the shape of a girl.

"Shelia?"

"Markaza!" Once the glowing figure fully materialized, Shelia wrapped her arms around her friend and squeezed.

Markaza's breath whooshed out of her as she held tightly. They broke apart, and she smiled. "You look like a goddess."

Shelia giggled. "I feel so free!" She twirled with her arms extended, trails of glittery dust raining from her feet, a smile on her face. "This body doesn't remember any of the trauma the other one did. I'm finally at peace." When her gaze returned, she sobered. "But what are you doing here?"

It was a beautiful thing to see her free of the burden Melvin had put on her shoulders. "I ran toward your body, and I guess the thing got hold of me. I don't remember a lot besides digging up the dirt with my hands as I tried to stay out of that damned hole." Markaza shrugged. "Too late now, I suppose. Why didn't you listen?"

"I love you for caring. So much. But, Markaza, you're not supposed to be here." Shelia frowned, not answering the question.

"What do you mean?"

"It wasn't your time." She put her thumb on Markaza's face and caressed her cheek. A tendril of light moved from her face to her belly button. "You still have so much to do."

"I do? Then why am I here?" A curl of hope wound in Markaza's chest, tying around her heart, causing butterflies to beat their wings on her sternum. Hope that she could somehow find a way back, it wasn't really over, and she'd have the chance to marry the man she was bananas over filled her. She fingered her ring and sighed.

"I don't know. But if they get to you in time, it may not be the end."

Those pesky flying bugs flapped harder. "What does that mean?" Her voice faded near the end of the question.

"I love you, Markaza. Be okay. I'm happy now. There's no greater sacrifice than giving your own life to save another. I was given another chance." Shelia flickered and then disappeared.

Everything went back to black with no sensation. "What? Shelia!" Markaza screamed. "Shelia! Don't go! I don't understand." A tugging began in her stomach that felt as though a tiny wire had been guided through her belly button, run through her spine, and handed to someone who was told to pull. It grew to a painful, jerking sensation. She gasped, wishing she could feel air moving into her lungs in the strange black place. Her eyes rolled back in her head from the pain, and she groaned.

"There she is! Keep going. She's coming around."

It sounded like Melody's voice, but Markaza couldn't be sure. Someone was striking her chest, and she heard a rib crack.

She coughed.

Coughed! Her eyes flew open, lungs sucking in sweet oxygen, and she threw her hand out to stop the assault on her torso. More coughing and gasping.

Strong arms surrounded her, lifting her from the ground. Richard's face swam into focus, his eyes fixed forward as he strode toward an ambulance waiting nearby.

"Richard?" She rasped.

He stopped and looked down at her. "Shh… I'm taking you to the ambulance. Let me pay attention so I don't trip, okay?"

Her head moved up and down.

They continued.

Once she was on a gurney, he grabbed her hand and smiled. "Babe, you're filthy."

It was difficult, but she managed a wan smile in return. Eyelids that felt like they had weights attached to them tried to slide closed. She fought to stay alert.

Richard stared at her hand, his fingers caressing hers. When he spoke again, he had to keep clearing his throat. "You scared me. I thought I'd lost you."

"What happened?" she whispered.

"I guess something knocked me out. When I came to, your head was disappearing over the edge of the pit. I ran toward you, but Bronya pushed me down." He scratched at the back of his neck. "What those women did next was nothing short of awesome."

"Tell me."

"I've never seen anything like it. If I hadn't seen it, I would never have believed it. I don't even know how to describe it so you'd understand."

"Try."

He took a deep breath and exhaled, working his eyebrows against one another and scratching his chin. "Well, there was this white light thing that came up out of the tar. It looked like a… I can't believe I'm about to say this…" His eyes were wide.

"Just say it."

"An Ent."

"A what?"

A frustrated breath escaped his lips. "You know, those things in that movie you love? The tree guys? *Lord of the Rings*?"

She nodded.

"Well, this one didn't have creepy eyes or a mouth, but it came up out of that mucky stuff, and those girls jumped on the limbs and *rode* it under the surface. When they crawled back out—without the Ent thing—they had you with them, tied by the middle with some white vine stuff." His eyelashes fluttered, and he shook his head. "You weren't breathing, so I started CPR. Now, here we sit."

Mysterious creatures glowing with white light, rising from the ground at the call of a bunch of chicks with weird abilities? Markaza snorted. She knew far-fetched, and that was *way* outside the realm of her imagination. But she'd seen the white apparition. Only, when it appeared the first time, it resembled the demon they were fighting.

Unable to keep her eyes open, she allowed sleep to embrace her. As she was drifting off, she heard Richard say, "By the way, I don't know if you can still hear me, but Shelia didn't make it."

Markaza smiled.

CHAPTER TWENTY-FIVE

RECOVERY

Beep!

Beep!

Beep!

The heart monitor kept up a steady rhythm, making music with the ticks of the second hand of the clock on the wall.

"Shut up! You did not."

Giggles.

"Shh! You guys are gonna wake her up."

"Sorry."

Markaza inhaled deeply through her nose, gathering the pure oxygen flowing into her lungs from the tube resting on her top lip. "Wake who? Because I'm already up." She grinned. "I've been listening to you guys whispering for the last hour." One by one, she cracked open her eyes.

All the guys and girls were piled in the room, some sitting on the chair—two perched on the arms and one in the actual seat—some on the floor, and one on the end of Markaza's bed.

Her leg got a light slap from Melody. "You tick-turd. What did you hear?"

"I heard you talking about a party, and something about a wedding, and…" Markaza's thoughts went into racecar mode. "Hey, did I hear mention of a baby shower?" She sat up and panned her eyes around the room, studying each of her friends for a hint.

Lily was snuggled up in Kurt's lap, her face flushed. She nodded when her eyes met Markaza's.

"Oh my God! Congratulations, you guys!" Moving hurt like the hounds of Hell were trying to rip her limb from limb, but she extended her arms for a hug anyway.

Lily turned crimson. "No! Not us!"

Markaza deflated and dropped her arms. "Who then?"

"You."

Richard was grinning from ear to ear and nodding.

"But, how? We were so careful." She looked down at her belly and gingerly touched it with her fingertips. "I'm gonna be a mother." It came out as a whisper, though she didn't mean to say it aloud at all.

Bronya squealed and clapped—so out of character for her. "Isn't it great?"

Markaza collapsed in a sobbing pile of misery. She wasn't even sure how to care for herself, much less take responsibility for a whole other life. As another revelation popped into her head, she gasped. "I'm not married!" She jerked her head up.

Everyone was looking at her like she'd just strangled a puppy.

"What?"

"Aren't you happy?" Bronya asked.

Am I happy? Rather than answer, Markaza stared. She wasn't sure what she was. Terrified, that was one thing. Confused, that was for sure. But happy? Happy to be bringing a child into such a screwed up world, always wondering if you're going to mess them up for life, and constantly worried something will happen to them? How anyone was ever happy about that at such a young age, she couldn't understand.

Coralie's eyes were full of worry and understanding. She got up off the floor and sat down on the bed, taking her friend's hand. "I know what you're thinking. It's too soon, right?"

Markaza nodded and sucked in her bottom lip.

"It's okay to be happy. Hell, it's okay to be excited. This is gonna be an adventure, and you have us by your side to help you through it." Coralie smiled. "You're gonna have a baby with the man you love. One who's been through the wringer with you and wanted to marry you before all this stuff happened. How a man wouldn't be completely smitten with you after knowing you for more than five minutes is a mystery. Heck, even Bronya has a bit of a crush on you."

Markaza lifted a brow at Bronya.

She shrugged and gave a lopsided grin.

"What I'm saying is, you have friends willing to hold your hair back when you puke, help you when you drop your keys and can't bend over to pick them up, rub your feet when they swell, and make sure your baby has the best of the best. And you have a wonderful man by your side who adores you. There's a lot to be happy about. It's okay. Be happy." Coralie laughed and hugged Markaza.

As she melted into the embrace, she started to believe the words. They rubbed her aching heart and massaged peace into the thumping organ. A breeze floated through the room and caressed her cheek.

"Oh, and don't worry. We plan to have your wedding as soon as you can walk out of here," Lily said.

Markaza jerked her head around. "What?"

Lily was nodding vigorously. "Your mother is already ordering stuff."

"My… Wait, my mom?"

"Yup. She went all crazy grandma when the doctors told her. Said she was positive it was gonna be a girl, and was mumbling something about shopping and construction as she hoofed it outta here," Bronya said. "She's freakin' thrilled."

Again, Markaza directed her attention to her stomach. Just below her navel, a tiny light flickered for just a moment. She smiled and cupped her growing baby in her hand.

Richard moved to her side and put his hand on top of hers. "I can't say I meant to have a baby, but I'm sure glad it's gonna be with you. I love you, babe. Let's have an adventure together."

What she was positive was a wacky grin split her face as she looked up at him. "Hell yes."

Bronya grabbed the television remote and pressed the button while shushing everyone. "Here it is!"

A newscaster's flawless face filled the screen. "It's a sad day here in the city. Last night, in Central Park, there were rumors of an accident that took the lives of many New Yorkers. According to eyewitnesses, Great Hill exploded, sending shrapnel and hot tar through the surrounding area, killing forty-five, and injuring seventy-six when an apartment building on Madison Avenue was destroyed. Firefighters continue their search through the rubble for dead and wounded.

"But, out of this tragedy comes the story of a heroine. A young woman by the name of Shelia Morgan was identified as the person responsible for saving countless lives. We were told by a source in the police department that Shelia was in the park when the ground started to erupt, and put herself in harm's way to warn the people on Madison Avenue. Luckily, she was able to clear three blocks before the explosion took place. The coroner's report says the cause of death was renal failure, and she died instantly."

A picture of Shelia appeared on the screen near the announcer's face.

"Recently, Ms. Morgan was one of the sponsors behind the I Heart New York campaign for raising awareness. People close to her say she was a kind, giving person, who would've given her last pair of shoes to someone that needed them.

"Well done, Ms. Morgan. You're a true heroine, and the city of New York applauds you for your outstanding act of bravery.

"In other news, the apocalypse everyone has been preparing…"

Melody snatched the remote and clicked the off button.

There wasn't a dry eye in the room.

Chapter Twenty-Six

Life and Death

A funeral was held for Shelia two weeks later, right after Markaza was released from the hospital. It turned out to be a serendipitous trip. Kurt got to talking with some of the staff while she was there and had been offered a position—which he took right away.

Everyone was gathered around the gravesite watching the men in coveralls throw dirt on the coffin.

Johanna was inconsolable. She was leaning heavily on Bronya and wailing like a banshee. Every now and again, the keening would stop to be replaced with a string of whys and many unrepeatable curses at God for picking the most brilliant flower in his garden.

Markaza never told anyone about her experience in the dark. She kept the memory of those last moments close to her heart and recalled them when she felt like she might cry. Over and over, the others asked her if she was okay, and if there was something she wasn't telling them, but she'd just nod and say she was fine, giving them a Mona Lisa smile. Finally, they quit asking.

As the motley crew walked back to their cars, Melody asked the question Markaza had been waiting for. "Did anyone call her aunt?"

She ticked her head to one side. "I put Kim on the job, but he came up empty handed. I'm not sure she would've wanted her aunt here, anyway."

"Oh. Yeah, maybe not. Good point."

They walked in silence the rest of the way, hugging briefly before dispersing to their vehicles. Drivers scurried to open doors.

Coralie and Bronya were going straight to the airport to get on a plane bound for Houma, Louisiana, so she could see her grammy one more time before the old woman passed. They'd gotten word she was in the hospital, and the doctors didn't think she'd last more than a couple of weeks.

When Bronya heard, she'd grinned. "I bet she'll be kickin' it for another fifteen years just to prove them wrong. She's a tough old bird."

There'd been talk of a trip to New Orleans for the two girls, and they planned to raise some hell in coonass country before returning to New York.

Melody and Walt were making a trip to Atlantic City to blow off some steam. He'd been coming around a lot since their date, and got all starry-eyed every time he looked at her.

Kurt and Lily were going apartment hunting.

Markaza had offered them a suite at The Clementine, but they'd declined, saying they needed time to get to know one another as a couple.

Richard put his arm around Markaza and pulled her close. "They'll be back, you know. Our wedding's just two months away, and then there's your baby shower in July. Once our little muffin graces the world with his—or her—presence, we'll have to beat them out of the apartment with a stick.

She smiled. "You think?"

"I *know*." He kissed her forehead. "Plus, you and Lily have a wedding to plan. You're gonna be sick of her soon."

"I'm not sure that's possible."

"I hope not, babe." His hand snaked over to rest on top of hers, both of them cradling the baby. "This kid is gonna be so spoiled."

Tears of joy sprang up in her eyes. "Yeah, how many kids get actual fairy godmothers?"

He slapped his leg and laughter boomed through the car.

"Oh, driver?" She gave Richard a wicked smirk. "Would you mind going to this address?" It was rattled off and the man nodded.

"Where's that?"

"You'll see. It's something I think is appropriate for the situation."

***

Markaza rolled over and snuggled close to Richard. She lifted a hand and touched his face—so angelic while he was sleeping. Eyes without creases, jaw slack, and even breath; he was so sweet. Gently, she leaned over and kissed his eyelids. "Wake up."

He groaned and swatted at her. "Five more minutes."

A devil perched on her shoulder, and she shoved her cold hands under the blanket, running them up his warm back.

Laughing, he ensnared her in a hug, flipped her over, and pinned her down with her arms over her head. "Woman!"

With her bottom lip captured between her teeth, she smiled. Then, she pulled what she hoped came off as a concerned face. "Was it cold, sweetheart?"

He growled and tickled her until she was gasping. "That's for waking me up."

She quirk-smirked at him. "Don't you know why I woke you?"

"No. Tell me." His lips crashed into hers.

Heat flowed through her face from the point of contact. When he broke and leaned back, she said, "It's February twenty-third. Today's our wedding day."

Richard wiggled his eyebrows. "And that means we have to get up early?"

"You don't, but I have a ton of stuff to do today, and I didn't want to leave without a kiss and telling you goodbye."

They kissed again, tongues dancing against one another in a waltz, until they were both panting. Markaza's body burned where it pressed against his.

"You better get out of here, babe. I'm not sure you'll be going anywhere if we keep doing that."

"True. Save it for later, stud muffin." Cackling burst out of her as she fled her bedroom.

Lily was waiting in the kitchen, cup of coffee extended.

Markaza snagged the coffee, slurped, and let out a sigh of contentment. "So, General Lily, what's on the agenda for today?"

"First, you're going to get dressed." Lily looked her friend up and down and smirked. "Don't put makeup on! The ladies at the salon will do that. They're our first stop. Then, it's off to the church."

"Yeah, and I'm driving."

With a jump, Markaza spun around, her hand flying up to cover her heart. "Don't *dooo* that! You scared the shit outta me!"

Johanna stood up and bowed. "My apologies, madam." Head to toe, she was covered in white. Hat, shoes, jacket, and pants were all bleached spotless. Her blouse was sparkling silver, refracting the light in a rainbow of brilliance that danced off the walls.

"Wow. You clean up nice, Mama!" Markaza wolf whistled.

212

They only got to hug for a moment before Lily started shooing Markaza down the hall. "Go! We're gonna be late!"

With a skip in her step, she sauntered to the bathroom to change and brush her hair and teeth. Oral-B sticking out of her mouth, she studied her calf. In honor of Shelia, Markaza had gotten her leg tattoo right after the funeral. It stood out against her creamy complexion, the delicate flowers and vines climbing up her leg, entwined with an octopus trying to drag them down, reminding her beauty could still exist within chaos.

Richard had been such a chicken about the pain, but she'd talked him into getting something small. He'd settled on a geometric tree with a bird bursting from the trunk on his bicep.

She smiled, spit, rinsed her mouth, and looked back into her own eyes. "Today's the day. Goodbye, purple!"

Squealing, she raced back down the hall and out the door with Lily and Johanna in tow.

At the salon, they met up with Bronya, Coralie, and Melody. Everyone was talking at once, enjoying the pampering and prepping for the big day while they caught up on news.

Bronya and Coralie had visited Bourbon Street while in Louisiana, and they told stories about the people and atmosphere there that made Markaza's hair stand on end.

Coralie slapped her leg. "You've never seen anything like it! They have drive-through places that sell mixed drinks!"

"Really? Is that legal?" Markaza asked. "I wonder why I didn't come across one when I was there."

"Yes! They put a straw in the cup and stick a piece of tape over the top. Craziest thing I've ever seen. You probably missed it because we had to drive out of the way to get there."

"Wow."

Melody told stories of her and Walt, and she got all moony-eyed when she mentioned his name.

The other girls had fun teasing her and watching her makeup artist get frustrated when Melody's skin changed colors every few minutes.

Hours passed that way until they were all coiffed, buffed, polished, and prettified. Then, it was into the limo and the final ride to the church.

Markaza's hands and feet wouldn't stay still.

"You okay?" Lily looked pointedly at the vibrating limbs.

"Oh. Ha! Yeah. I'm just nervous, I guess."

"Everything's going to be just fine."

"I hope so." Markaza tried to still her ticks, but her heart was racing, and she had no idea why. It wasn't as if she was scared he wouldn't show up, or was unsure about what life with him would be like. Still, a viper of fear writhed in her belly. Then, an orange light flickered through the interior of the car, and the most relaxing feeling filled her up. She sighed and smiled, knowing there was an angel of a woman watching, protecting, and making sure everything was as it should be.

Fidgeting with the veil while waiting for the doors to open, Markaza admired the flowers woven into the fabric draped over her hair. They were lilies, and were tinted orange, yellow, green, blue, pink, and silver. She felt her girls with her, even though they'd already walked down the aisle and were waiting at the other end with her future husband.

Husband.

Her pinky finger on her right hand rubbed her belly. All of a sudden, she felt a flutter behind her belly button. Love encompassed her soul with warm arms and a steady breath. "Well, hello there, baby. What an interesting time for you to make your first move."

With a flourish, the heavy wooden doors opened, and her eyes riveted to the man in the tux she was about to make her forevermore. "How about we go marry your daddy?"

THE MYSTIC

***

Four months later, Richard had Markaza blindfolded and was leading her down the hall to their apartment. It was the same one where she'd lived with the girls, but it had been remodeled to fit a growing family rather than six single women. She hadn't seen it yet, and he refused to let her back in while the work was being done, claiming it was too dangerous. As she thought about it, she chuckled under her breath. *Dangerous. Who does he think he's kidding?*

"Something funny, babe?"

"No. I was just thinking about how amazing you are."

"And that made you laugh?"

"Yes. It did."

"Care to tell me why?" His tone was teasing, egging her on like he always did.

"No. I think I'll keep it to myself."

"You're so frustrating, but I wouldn't have you any other way. You do know that, right?"

She nodded once. "Absolutely."

With a gentle tug, he pulled her to a stop and turned her to the right. She heard the door click open, and he guided her forward a couple of steps before stopping her again.

"You ready to see it?" he asked.

"Yes!" Instantly, a delicious smell hit her full force. "Oh my God! Do I smell cake?"

"Wow. Can't trick the pregnant lady." He pulled off the blindfold.

"Surprise!" Bronya, Lily, Melody, Coralie, Kurt, Walt, and Markaza's mother all screamed in unison.

Mouth hanging open wide enough to catch flies, Markaza stood, stunned, as she took in the new apartment. It was designer everything, but decorated with sugar skull artwork, tribal pieces, and oriental flare. It screamed her name, and she couldn't move. Everything was draped in streamers and ribbon, and a huge cake decorated like a sugar skull sat on the table.

Startling her out of the trance, the baby kicked, and she rubbed her stomach as her gaze moved to her friends. "Yeah, pretty awesome, huh? Mommy has the best friends in the world, and she's lucky to have your daddy."

Richard was beaming. "You like it?"

She shook her head.

His face fell. "You don't?"

"No. I freaking *love* it! It's so perfect!"

He lit back up. "Before you get to the party, there's one more thing I want to show you."

"There's more?" She squealed.

One hand on her lower back, he guided her to the sitting room and pointed at the wall. There, in a beautifully carved silver frame, was the picture from Coralie's birthday party with all six women. Markaza's hand flew to her mouth as she took in the glamor, radiance, and Shelia's beautiful face, smiling. Tears welled in Markaza's eyes as she spun around, threw her arms around his neck, and kissed him like he might disappear at any moment.

When they broke apart, he was grinning like the cat who ate the canary. "Wow. If that's my thanks, I'll surprise you more often."

Through her tears, she chuckled and smacked his arm. "I kiss you like that all the time."

"Well, we'll just say that was the best one yet." He winked.

She could feel her face burning. "Okay, let's get to the party already!"

Her friends cheered and gathered around, chatting and drinking coffee while the gifts were opened. When it was time to cut the cake, Lily leapt from her seat and waved an envelope in the air. "Wait!" she yelled. "First, we're gonna reveal the sex of the baby!"

THE MYSTIC

Bronya shushed everyone. "Go ahead, Markaza."

Lily handed over the secret paperwork and stood there, hovering, bouncing on her toes.

With deliberately slow movements, Markaza stuck her finger under the flap and peeled back the adhesive. When she got close to the end, she looked up and smiled.

"Oh, stop teasing me! Open it already!"

She wasn't sure if she wanted it to be a boy or a girl, and she wasn't sure she even cared. Richard had said numerous times he'd like to have a son but would love a daughter just as much, so they hadn't really settled on what they were *hoping* for. Before Markaza pulled out the paper, she made up her mind. As long as the baby was healthy, the sex didn't matter.

Jerking the card free, she held it up without looking.

Gasps filled the room, and everyone clapped.

Slowly, her eyes traveled up her arm to her hand until they reached the bright pink and orange striped card extended above her head.

Richard yelled, "It's a girl!"

There was much hugging, oohing, and ahhing.

Bronya clapped her hands. "Okay, I don't know about the rest of you, but I'm dying for information over here." She looked around dramatically. "What are you gonna name her?"

Markaza smiled and intertwined her fingers over her belly, pressing her palms into the bulge there. The baby kicked, eliciting a loving smile from its mother.

"I'm going to name her Shelia Pamela Deveaux."

The End

(or is it?)

Books in this series:

The Fury
The Visionary
The Beguiler
The Siren
The Prophet
The Mystic

Dear Readers,

Thank you for sticking with me for so long. I appreciate it more than you'll ever know! These stories mean a lot to me (as you know if you've been with me from the start), and I hope you take the tales to heart.

And, to those of you who sent me messages about Marka-za, thank you, too. It meant a lot that you were invested in the story and wanted to know more!

Yes, there's evil and hate in the world, but there's also good. Let it start with you. Go out today and smile at someone, make a goofy face at that baby in the store, tell a friend how much he or she means to you, or give your significant other one more hug. Pay it forward. Karma is always watching, and you never know what tomorrow will bring.

Mindset is half the battle.

May your days be full of fluffy, colorful things and many hugs,

Jo

Acknowledgements:

First and foremost, I have to send a huge hug and lots of love to my husband. Without him, none of this would've been possible. He indulges my dreams and supports me so much in my endeavors. I'd truly be lost without him. So, thank you, Mike. You're the light of my life and the beat of my heart, and I love you so very much. The day I met you was the first day of the rest of my life, and I wouldn't trade it for the world.

My mom has been chomping at the bit for each book in this series. Seriously, if she hadn't stayed on me, I'm not sure I would've continued after the first one. Thanks, Mom, for loving these ladies as much as I do, and thanks for being so invested in their stories. My love of literature comes from you, and I count myself lucky to have embraced it at such a young age. Thanks for that, too!

I have a friend unlike any other. She's been my backbone when mine melted, the shoulder I cry on, and the person I turn to when I need to vent about anything. On top of that, she's the partner in my business venture, INDIE Books Gone Wild. Anytime I have a question of whether we should do X, Y, or Z, I ask her and our thoughts are in line. It's bizarre. I call her my sister from another mister. Tia, I hope you have an inkling of how much I appreciate you. Without your help, I'd be a lost ship at sea, waiting to be tumbled by the storm. Thank you from the bottom of my heart for being you and for being my friend. Not sure how you picked this crazy chick from all others in that blog challenge to befriend, but you're a blessing.

Thank you to all the readers! Without you reading my books, why would I bother writing them? If I touched any of your lives in any way, I count myself lucky. It makes me so happy to hear how my stories connect with people, and brings even more light into my life. I'm a lucky duck to have each and every one of you! Know you're appreciated!

Last on this list of thanks goes a vibrant young lady who fell in love with my series and got to pre-read this novel for continuity before I sent it for editing. Jackie. Girl, what would I have done without your insight? You really helped me find the holes, and this story is so much better from your notes. I adore you so much. I can't wait to see you soon. Thank you for all your help, thank you for loving my ladies, and thank you for your outright honesty.

WSTW!
WOMEN WILL SAVE THE WORLD!

About the Author

Jo Michaels loves writing novels that make readers gasp in horror, surprise, and disbelief. While her browser search history has probably landed her on a list somewhere, she still dives into every plot with gusto, hoping "the man" will realize she's a writer and not a psychopath about to go on a rampage. Her favorite pastimes are reading, watching Investigation Discovery, and helping other authors realize their true potential through mentoring. She's penned the award-winning Pen Pals and Serial Killers series and the best-selling educational book for children, Writing Prompts for Kids, which has rocketed the kids that use it into several awards of their own.

Most of Jo's books feature the places she's lived: Louisiana, Tennessee, and Georgia. That's given her a special amount of insight to what makes those locations tick. Her works are immersive and twisty, and she wouldn't want it any other way.

More Books by Jo Michaels

<u>(Middle Grade Titles)</u>
The Abigale Chronicles 1, 2, and 3

<u>Young Adult Titles</u>
The Frivolity Fairies: A Christmas Short Story FREE
M (Sci-Fi)
I, Zombie (Horror)
The Bird (Romance)
Fractured Glass: A Novel Anthology (Sci-Fi)
War and Pieces ~ Frayed Fairy Tales (Season 1: Episode 1 is FREE – grab it here)
Black Tie Christmas (Romance)

<u>New Adult Titles</u>
Faye Magic – Othala Witch Collection - Sector 16 – Standalone (PNR)
Utterances (Contemporary Fantasy)
<u>12/21/12 Series (Apocalyptic Fiction)</u>
The Fury
The Visionary
The Beguiler
The Siren
The Prophet
The Mystic

<u>Adult Titles</u>
<u>Pen Pals and Serial Killers Series (Psychological Thrillers)</u>
Emancipation
Provocation
Intensification
The House (a killer collection of short stories to tie up the PPSK series)

Innocent (Psychological Thriller)
Yassa: Genghis Khan's Coming-of-age Tale (Historical)
7: The Seven Deadly Sins (Historical Fantasy)

<u>Non-fiction Titles</u>
Writing Prompts for Kids
Writing Prompts for Teens
The Indie Author's Guide to: Building a Great Book
How to be a TOTAL LOSER and feel better than you ever have
War and Pieces ~ Frayed Fairy Tales – Coloring Book of Shoes

www.ingramcontent.com/pod-product-compliance
Lightning Source LLC
Chambersburg PA
CBHW051050050726

47592CB00002B/462